THE ESCORT NEXT DOOR

Copyright © 2013 by Clara James

This is a work of fiction. Names, characters, places, and incidents either are the product of the author's imagination or are used fictitiously, and any resemblance to any persons, living or dead, business establishments, events, or locales is entirely coincidental.

The Escort Next Door

All rights reserved.

This book is protected under the copyright laws of the United States of America. No part of this work may be used, reproduced, or transmitted in any form or by any means, electronic or mechanical, including photocopying, recording and faxing, or by any information storage and retrieval system by anyone but the purchaser for their own personal use.

This book may not be reproduced in any form without the express written permission of Clara James, except in the case of a reviewer who wishes to quote brief passages for the sake of a review written for inclusions in a magazine, newspaper, or journal—and these cases require written approval from Clara James prior to publication. Any reproduction or other unauthorized use of the material or artwork herein is prohibited without the express written permission of the author.

Fonts used with permission from Microsoft

Also by bestselling author

Clara James

~The Escort Next Door Series~

The Escort Next Door

The Escort Next Door: Captivated

The Escort Next Door: Escape

~Her Last Love Affair Series~

Her Last Love Affair

Her Last Love Affair: Breathing Without You

Her Last Love Affair: The Final Journey

To view these titles visit:
http://amzn.to/15ek5q7

Chapter One

TIME WITH FRIENDS

Paul and I had known Ben and Linda for a long time, long enough to make me feel 'old'. In fact, it was through us that the pair met. Linda had been a close friend of mine when we were both part-time clerks in an accountancy firm. She was working her way through college; I was expecting my first child.

Ben on the other hand was a friend of Paul's, they'd met in the gym and often played basketball together. Ben and Linda were eventually brought together when Paul and I threw a housewarming party. The rest as they say, is history.

"Why don't we do this more often?" Linda asked, as she offered to refill my wine glass.

"No, thanks," I politely declined. "I guess life just gets in the way," I added in response to her other question. Life really had gotten in the way, it had been over eighteen months since we'd seen Ben and Linda and in that time, we'd moved again; Paul's father had retired and Paul had taken over as CEO of the family business.

"I can imagine how busy you've been," she chuckled.

"You don't know the half of it," Paul chimed in. He was reaching for his own full glass and leaning causally back in his chair. His scarlet tie had been pulled loose enough for him to undo the top button of his shirt. The jacket of his charcoal suit had long since been removed and draped across the back of the chair. I tried to remember the last time I'd seen him that relaxed, but couldn't. He smiled broadly, that grin that never failed to light up the room. "You know, I thought life would be easier not harder once I was the boss," he added, the index finger of his free hand rubbing at his temple.

Ben laughed loudly, looping his hand over the back of Linda's chair and gently caressing her upper arm with the tips of his fingers. "I'm glad," he managed to blurt. "If being the owner of a multimillion dollar company is a walk in the park, then you're going to make me vomit."

The Escort Next Door

Paul's laugh was muted, but he did shrug good-naturedly at Ben's teasing. "You're doing all right," he added, a touch defensively.

Ben tossed his bright blue eyes to Linda and they shared a silent smile. Eventually, he turned his attention back to my husband and nodded. "We're getting by. There are things I'd like to do, though," he added, his fingers stroking the stem of his wine glass. "I'd love to be able to treat Linda more. You know, I mean you can just whisk Julia away whenever, wherever. Money's never an issue."

"Yeah," Paul acknowledged, "money isn't the issue; it's time." As he shifted his left leg, his knee brushed mine and, even after almost fourteen years together, I felt a spark of electricity.

My face tipped towards his and I wondered if he felt it too. However, there was nothing in his face or his eyes that gave it away. Instead, he continued talking about how insanely busy he always is and the fact that he spends half his time traveling. I was tempted to correct him to three quarters of the time, but it seemed like a petty remark and I knew it would only anger him.

"That must be tough," Linda said sympathetically. "But you guys are such a strong couple," she added brightly. "I don't know anyone else who's still happily married to their high school sweetheart."

I smiled at her, before turning that grin on Paul. His eyes however were drawn to his glass, which he quickly drained.

We'd been sixteen, both starting our junior year, when I moved schools. At the time, I'd thought it was the worst thing that had ever happened to me. I distinctly remember hating my parents that summer. But in my very first class at my brand new school, I met Paul. I knew nothing about him, had no idea about his family business or how wealthy his parents were. All I knew was he was the most handsome guy I'd ever seen. Dark hair and deep brown eyes, tall, athletic, with a warm smile. The more I learned, the more I liked. He wasn't just a pretty face or a mindless jock, he had a brain too.

I, on the other hand, had issues. I was a bit too thin, a lot too flat-chested, ignored by the popular crowd and socially quite awkward. I'd felt sure that Paul didn't even know I existed. Little did I know that he had, indeed, been taking an interest in me. It wasn't until years later that he confessed to sneaking peaks at me during rehearsals with the dance team. Anyway, at the time, I was oblivious and so completely shocked when he asked me out on a date.

Those years had been magical, I was so in love with this man and giddy at the realization that he felt

The Escort Next Door

the same way. It was like every single one of those teenage romances I'd seen in the movies.

"I think it's wonderful," Linda commented, pulling me from my memories.

"Yeah," I agreed, nodding. "It is wonderful." Another glance at Paul found him examining the desert menu. "I mean, I know it's old fashioned," I added, "but I love that Paul is and always will be the only one."

"Hmm," he hummed in reply, his eyes still staring at the menu.

Giving up on attempts to get his attention, my own face dropped catching a glimpse of the cleavage that had been enlarged by three pregnancies. In many ways, I was physically more attractive than I had been at sixteen; my boyish figure now had some womanly curves, my breasts were significantly bigger and I felt much more comfortable in my skin. Wasn't that supposed to exude confidence and make me glow? Perhaps the problem was, I didn't feel very confident. Although I liked what I saw in the mirror, Paul always seemed to look right through me.

I'm not naïve enough to expect champagne and roses. I realize that the realities of day-to-day life don't lend themselves to the romance of teenage fantasies. There were other more important things; business trips to go on; a mortgage to pay; children to look after. I just wished that didn't mean my relationship with Paul had to come last on the list.

"Anyway," I sighed, suddenly feeling uncomfortable with the silence. "How are things at work?" I asked.

Linda nodded as she swallowed a mouthful of wine and replaced her glass on the table. "It's busy," she replied. "I've got two new clients and I'm trying to wrangle a good deal for them both." After studying literature at college, Linda had toyed with writing for a year or so. Eventually, she'd decided that she wanted to try something different and became a literary agent. A choice that turned out to be incredibly lucrative for her. "I'm thinking of slowing down a bit, though," she added.

"Really?" I asked, confused. I knew she loved her job and also knew that she and Ben were saving to build their own beachfront property.

"Yeah," she said, turning to her husband as if seeking permission. Ben gave no obvious sign one way or the other, but Linda could clearly read something in his eyes that I couldn't, because she grinned before gabbling, "We're trying for a baby."

"Oh," I smiled. "That's great."

"We've been thinking about it a lot lately," Ben offered, with a broad grin of his own. "We see you two with your little family and we just think..." he inhaled slowly, trying to find the right words. "Well, we want that too," he sighed.

I tried to smile, feeling instantly guilty for my rather self-pitying thoughts. What Paul and I had was enviable. I was in an enviable position, I had no business wishing things were different. "Well, I'm sure you'll make wonderful parents," I said.

Noticing Paul move out of the corner of my eye, I turned my face and watched him lift his glass, which now only had a small swill of red wine in the bottom. "Enjoy all that sex while you can, man," he joked, offering the glass toward Ben.

Ben laughed heartily tapping his own glass to Paul's. "Thanks," he chuckled.

Linda giggled too, her slender arm snaking around Ben's neck as she leaned in and kissed him on the cheek. "It's exciting," she blurted, turning back to me and leaving a red lipstick print on her husband's face.

I guessed she was expecting a reply, but with a false grin plastered on my face, I couldn't help but turn Paul's remark over and over in my mind. On the one hand, I wondered if I was being oversensitive. On the other, I felt that he'd taken a very personal swipe at me in front of our friends. Maybe, I silently suggested, his poor attempt at humor is nothing more than a bit of bravado. After all, I'm not the one that seems to have lost an interest in sex. He's always shunning any kind of intimacy, because he's 'too tired', or he 'has to get up early in the morning' or 'one of the children might walk in'.

"It's crazy to think that you were pregnant with Lizzie when we first met," Linda continued. "And she's what now? Seven?"

"Eight in a couple of months," I replied, automatically. I'd been unaware of even processing what she'd said let alone formulating a reply.

"Ahh," she cooed. "Next time we meet up, you'll have to bring the kids along, too."

"Yeah," Ben agreed. "It's been far too long since we've seen them. And I'm willing to bet that Dylan's becoming quite the little football player."

Our son was four going on forty. Bright and precocious, he had such an adult view of life. He takes after his father in many ways and had already decided that he wanted to be a professional athlete. Which sport, he was yet to decide. He told me that he needed to grow into his body to find out what he'd be best suited to.

"That's the difficult thing about being away for days and sometimes weeks at a time," Paul said, tossing the desert menu to one side and joining the conversation fully. "Every time I come back, they've all grown so much. Especially little Kate," he adds, shaking his head in disbelief. "One minute she was a baby, now she's a toddler already."

"They must miss you when you're away," Linda offered warmly.

"We all do," I replied, turning my eyes on him and, for the first time that night, receiving some recognition from him.

He flashed me a quick grin, and I momentarily saw the man I'd fallen in love with. It's those precious seconds that I treasured. Those were the times when I knew that deep down he was still the same and, therefore, on some level at least, *we* must be the same. He opened his mouth as if he was about to say something, but the words were never spoken. Instead, he was interrupted by the waitress, who asked whether anybody wanted desert.

Linda, Ben and Paul eagerly turned to her and ordered. I had no appetite for it.

Chapter Two

Drunk

It was me that had to drive home, after Paul consumed another three glasses of wine and a small Scotch and soda. The journey was reasonably short and was passed in mostly silence. I tried to draw him into conversation, commenting on how nice it was to see them again and how happy they both seemed. However, all I received was a grunt of agreement or indifference – it was hard to tell which, perhaps it was a bit of both.

When we got home, he immediately headed upstairs. Leaving me to thank and pay the sitter. After showing her out and watching at the door to make sure she got to her car okay, I made my own way up the stairs. Turning left on the landing, I tiptoed down the hallway, checking on each of the children before finally retracing my steps and wandering into our bedroom.

Paul was sitting in the high-backed, antique chair in the corner. He was leaning back, his legs spread casually wide and swaying slightly. One elbow was perched on the mahogany arm of the chair, his head dropped against his fist. With drooping eyelids, he looked at me.

"Becky is worried she's done something to upset you," I muttered, tossing my purse on the dressing table and kicking my three-inch heels off.

"Why?" he asked.

"Because you walked right past her and didn't say a word," I explained frustrated that it was necessary for me to do so.

His head suddenly straightening, he leaned forward, resting both arms on his knees. "Come over here," he said, his voice rumbling deeply in his chest.

I turned to face him, my hand reaching for one of the oak poles at the foot of our four-poster bed. "Did you hear what I said?" I asked wearily, perching my free hand on my hip.

"Yeah, yeah," he replied dismissively, his fingers grabbing the loose knot of his tie and pulling it free. He left it hanging around his neck and unclasped a button on his shirt which revealed some of the silky smooth skin of his chest. "Now, get over here," he repeated, cocking his head.

"Paul," I sighed. "I like her, she's great with the kids and she's always been very accommodating when we've needed her at the last minute. I don't want to lose her."

He rolled his heavy eyes as dramatically as his sluggish movements would allow. "Don't you think you're overreacting," he muttered.

"What I think," I replied tartly, "is that you were incredibly rude."

"She's the hired help," he scoffed. "I don't have to be nice to her, I pay her."

Exhaling slowly, I realized I was getting nowhere fast and the conversation was bringing out a side of him that I found intensely unattractive. Releasing my hold on the bed, I swiveled on the ball of my feet and headed toward our en suite bathroom. I didn't get more than two steps before Paul objected.

"Hey, where are you going?"

"Getting ready for bed," I tossed over my shoulder, not bothering to turn around.

He must have been capable of moving much more quickly that I would have expected, because as I got to the door, his hand darted over my shoulder and slapped flat down on the hard wood.

Exasperated, I turned to face him. "What are you doing?"

"I don't want to fight about the stupid babysitter," he said, his voice pitched soft and a little lower than usual, while his eyes attempted to focus on me.

"Paul," I sighed, placing my hands on his chest and pushing gently.

"What?" he asked, his chocolaty gaze moving from my face and taking a leisurely trip down the length of my body.

If it hadn't been obvious before, what he wanted was very clear to me by that point. Something about the way he looked at me caused a dozen butterflies to flutter wildly in my stomach. However, another sensation, a much more stubborn one, refused to let me give into that feeling. "You don't get any sex any more, remember?" I snapped. "That's what happens when you have kids, right?"

His eyebrows moved wearily in their surprise. "What the hell are you talkin' about?" he said, louder than I think he'd intended but unable to control his volume.

Shoving a little harder at his chest, I coaxed him back a half-step. "You know what I'm talking about," I replied, brusquely. "Have you any idea how embarrassing that was for me?"

The Escort Next Door

Paul kept his hand on the door and refused to budge any further. "For Christ's sake," he muttered under his breath, before shaking his head incredulously. "That was just a joke. Come on, Ben and Linda knew I was only messing around."

"It's not just a joke though, is it?" I quickly replied. "When was the last time we made love?"

My question was met with silence, while his eyes searched the ceiling and his mind trawled his memory. "I don't know," he eventually huffed. "It's been a while. We've both been busy. And when we're not busy, we're having stupid arguments like this one."

"So, it's my fault?" I defensively blurted.

"That's not what I said," he insisted. "Why do you always twist my words?" His volume crept up another notch as he slammed his palm against the still closed bathroom door.

"Shhh," I quickly hissed. "You'll wake the kids."

Exhaling heavily through his nose, he was quiet for a few moments. When he spoke again, it was in deliberately muted tones. "Why are we doing this?"

I couldn't be sure whether the question was being asked of me or my breasts, and I waited for his bleary eyes to find mine once more. "I think," I sighed, my head rocking back and resting against the door. "I think, we're both a little stressed and tired. It's a rough patch," I added. That final phrase was spoken with more confidence than I felt in it. In truth, it was a hope that I'd been clinging to. As the weeks and months dragged on, the 'patch' got bigger and bigger. I was beginning to wonder if things would ever improve.

His Adam's apple jumped as he swallowed. "All I've been thinking about over the last hour is getting you back here and ripping your clothes off," he said, the fingers of his free hand suddenly snaking over my hip.

"That's because you're drunk," I informed him, allowing him to tug my lower half to him. My hips met his with a slight bump and I felt the warm swell of his groin pressed against my belly. The evening had been far from romantic. I didn't particularly want to make love with him right then. It was clear to all but the blind that alcohol had made him horny. Nothing else seemed to matter to him, not the fact that we'd been fighting, nor the fact that it had been almost two months since the last time we'd had sex.

"So what?" he replied darkly, as he moved his body against mine resulting in a surge of blood to his penis.

He was rock hard, his erection straining at the tented front of his pants. I wanted to stay mad; I *was* still mad. And yet, two long months without physical intimacy had taken its toll on me. My fingers trembled as an all too familiar warmth began to pool in my stomach and spread slowly southward. "Maybe," I mumbled, realizing my mouth had gone suddenly dry. "Maybe we should talk about this in the morning." As I tried to grapple some control over my desire, he continued to drive me to the edge.

Drawing his face close to mine, he teased my lips with his. Close enough to kiss me, he simply brushed his mouth against mine and pulled back as I instinctively leaned toward his lips. "I don't want to talk," he breathed, "now or in the morning." His fingers stroked their way over my hip and grasped my buttock forcefully.

I gasped as he tugged me closer, grinding his lower half against mine. My hands automatically shot up to his shoulders, regaining my balance. "Kiss me," I pleaded, my fingers twisting in the soft cotton of his shirt.

Paul's hand slipped quickly from the bathroom door and snaked around my waist. He turned me hurriedly, panting with need as he pressed his open mouth to mine. His tongue dove between my lips, exploring with deep thrusts and little finesse. He pushed me rapidly and I followed his direction, my bare feet sliding backwards on the smooth carpet until my legs met the bedstead. His momentum didn't stop, and the force of his weight sent me flopping onto my back.

I bounced on the soft mattress, releasing a muffled groan as his weight landed carelessly on top of me. "Mmm," I mumbled into his mouth. "Hey," I panted, jerking my head to one side and tearing my lips away from his. "Let's slow down a little, huh?" I suggested, my hands stroking over the broad, sinewy muscles in his back. "There's no rush," I whispered into his ear.

Either unable or unwilling to listen, Paul grunted as his hands slid down my thighs. Hooking the fingers of one hand beneath my left knee, he coaxed my legs apart. His other hand was busy with the hem of my dress, pushing it haphazardly up. "Oh, God. I need you," he groaned, nestling his hips between my legs and pushing his still clothed groin to my underwear-covered sex.

It had been a long time since Paul had been that frenzied and impetuous. It was flattering to know, even after all those years, he wanted me so desperately. So, I felt torn. On one hand, grateful for being made to feel sexy and desired. On the other, a sense that this was little more than a mad dash to sheath himself within me.

"Paul," I moaned, the weight of his chest pressing the air out of my lungs.

"That's right," he panted heavily, uncoordinated hands fumbling awkwardly with the clasp and zipper of his pants. "Say my name." Muttering curses under his breath, he edged his pants and underwear off his hips, stopping as soon as they'd reached his upper thighs. His erection now free, the soft flesh of its head rubbed along my inner thigh.

"Babe," I muttered, the open zipper of his pants digging uncomfortably into my leg. "Please."

Misinterpreting my plea or perhaps just too engrossed in his own mission, Paul's sloppy, drunken hands gripped the edges of my panties. "Ugh," he grunted, yanking at the fabric. The rip of white lace met his growl of aggression and the backs of his fingers briefly brushed my outer lips.

Unconsciously, my hips jerked in response, craving more of the same. But his hand was cruelly ripped away as quickly as it had been placed there. I was aroused, I did want him, but I wasn't ready for what came next.

Paul quickly adjusted himself, bracing his hands on the mattress either side of my waist before driving his hips forwards with a masculine bark of release.

I sucked in a breath, my fingernails digging into his back, as my body was quickly and ruthlessly speared. "Ahh," I wailed, my sex seeming to fight against the invasion. I tried to force myself to relax, to breathe slowly and allow my body to accept him, but it was all happening much too quickly. Any sensual and erotic thoughts I tried to conjure were immediately chased away when he began to pump fiercely. "Ouch," I yelped. "Paul, you're hurting me."

His lower half was soon slapping against mine in a rapid tattoo. He groaned and muttered, the friction of my unprepared channel apparently proving uncomfortable for him. "You're pussy is so...tight," he grunted haltingly, only a syllable being uttered on each thrust.

I was barely able to hear him. Everything around me was a blur. The only thing that had any clarity was the pain of each callous drive of his pelvis, which caused me to bite down hard on my lower lip to keep from screaming.

Amid the discomfort and the grateful awareness that at least it wouldn't last long, I remember wondering what the hell was going on. Sex with Paul had never been like this, even when he'd had a few too many drinks. Even when he was a teenager and orgasm was all he ever thought about, he'd never *used* my body like he did that night. It was as though I was with a stranger.

Forcing my gaze upward, I stared at his face. His eyes were squeezed shut, but if they'd been open he would have been staring at the wall straight in front of him. His features were tight with pained concentration. I'll never know exactly what he was concentrating on, but it definitely wasn't me. Sweat was beading on his forehead as he continued to lurch forwards, slamming his erection to the hilt with each viscous thrust. "Oh, yeah," he grunted. "You like that."

I drew in a deep breath, holding it while his movements lost their rhythmic pattern. The speed and depth started to grow erratic, until finally with a groan of, "Oh, shit!" he flopped forward and collapsed on top of me. His hips jerked and one leg spasmed as I felt his seed pulse into me in strong, hot bursts. That sensation, which had always been indicative of love, pleasure and the sharing of something primal suddenly made me feel sullied. I instantly felt guilty for feeling that way. After all, this was my husband, the man I loved with all my heart. Maybe the encounter had been lacking in romance and foreplay, but I'd still given him something special, which meant, by default, that what we'd done was special. At least, that's what I tried to tell myself, as my eyes flooded with scorching tears.

"Oh, God," Paul gasped, his breathing coming hard against my chest, as he leisurely lifted himself from me. "Ugh, fuck," he muttered, rolling to one side. As his flaccid penis slipped from me, some of his semen dripped onto my inner thigh and, within seconds, created a chill that quickly spread throughout my entire body.

As soon as his bulk was off me, I reached down and pulled my dress back to my knees. My trembling fingers remained there, clinging to the hem. Paul's left arm was lazily flopped over my waist and his foot, which was still in his black loafer, was draped clumsily across my calf. The rest of him was pressed face down into the mattress by my side.

"Paul," I said with a quiet, shaky voice.

The only response I received was the low rumble of a snore. Laying under what felt like an incredibly bright glare from our bedroom light, my eyes fixed wide on the clean, white ceiling above. Shell-shocked, the events of the previous few minutes played on a continuous loop. Everything about him, from the way he'd behaved to the way he'd spoken, seemed alien to me. How could the man I'd been sleeping with since I was eighteen have changed so dramatically? Was it the result of two months of abstinence; a build up of frustration coupled with the effects of alcohol?

Those questions rolled unanswered around my brain, but it was another that took center stage. What the hell had just happened? It beat at my head over and over, as I laid stunned into motionlessness. I couldn't even define what had passed between us. It hadn't been anything resembling love making, not by my interpretation of the phrase. The way he'd cruelly taken what he wanted regardless of my discomfort bordered on rape, but then again, I'd never said, "no" or asked him to stop. I may not have been particularly happy with what was going on, but I'd passively allowed it to happen. And that brought with it another uncomfortable realization: it wasn't just Paul who had acted out of character that night.

Chapter Three

Visitor

I didn't get any sleep, and eventually crawled off of the bed at around five while the sun was just beginning to create an amber glow on the carpet. I slipped out from under Paul, not needing to worry about waking him, as he continued to snore loudly.

Leaving the room, I went down the hall to use the main bathroom, not because I was particularly worried about disturbing my husband's sleep, but I needed some time to compose myself before actually confronting what had gone on the night before. At that moment, I didn't know what to say to him. I even wondered whether the hours spent stewing over it had made me lose all perspective.

Climbing into the shower, I quickly soaped my body noting a graze on my inner left thigh and freshly pinkish bruises on both hip bones. The bruises were obviously caused by the force of his own pelvis knocking against me, it took me a little longer to realize that the tiny teeth of his open zipper had cut into the delicate flesh of my thigh. None of those injuries was particularly sore though, and with the exception of a slight tenderness between my legs, I had no other physical reminders of the evening. Still, try as I might, I simply couldn't shake the sense that something had gone very wrong in my relationship with Paul.

It took me no more than ten minutes to wash my body and hair. I spent a further hour standing beneath the hot jets, trying to figure out how to broach the subject.

Wrapped only in a towel and with hair loose and dripping wet, I returned to the bedroom. Still face down on the bed, Paul didn't stir. As I stepped into a pair of jeans and threw on a T-shirt, I watched him breathing heavily. With his dark hair tussled, dress shirt creased and pants hanging disheveled at his hips, he was a mess. It became clear that he was drunker than I'd realized the night before. Would he even remember what had happened? If he did, I was sure he'd feel guilty.

The Escort Next Door

Taking a glance at the time, I wondered whether I should wake him. After just two days at home, he was about to head out of town again. A car was coming to pick him up at nine, so I tried to calculate how much time we'd have for a heart to heart before he left.

"Paul," I whispered gently from the foot of the bed.

He didn't move, even the pattern of his breathing remained the same.

"Paul," I repeated, a little louder this time. "It's-"

"Mom!"

Spinning at the sound of the wail that interrupted me, I sighed. I hesitated momentarily, but when it became obvious that even the shouts of our children would not wake him, I decided to leave Paul alone for the time being.

Leaving the bedroom and shutting the door quietly behind me, I was met with the distressed face of my little boy. He wasn't crying, but I could see he was only seconds away from doing so; his big brown eyes watery and lip wobbly. Seeing me, he ran down the hall.

"Mom," he whimpered, his arms spread wide.

Crouching so that I was on his eye level, I placed my finger to my lips. "Daddy's still sleeping," I hushed.

He flung his chubby little fingers around my neck and I automatically wrapped one arm around his legs. With his butt resting on my forearm, I groaned as I scooped him off the floor. "You're getting big," I told him in a whisper. "I'm not going to be able to do this much longer."

He paid no attention, his legs quickly fastening around my waist and his face disappearing in my shoulder. I only managed to take him the few feet to his own room, before he was slipping down my hip. Carefully, I lowered him to the floor, sinking to his height as I did so.

"Now," I sighed, still in a hushed voice. "What's the matter?"

"Lizzie," he sniveled, pointing into his room.

When it became clear that was all I was going to get from my son, I stood up and stepped inside the room. All seemed normal, until I caught sight of an armless bear at the bottom of his bed. Stepping forwards, I scooped up the injured toy and turned to Dylan. "Did she do this?" I demanded.

With a trembling bottom lip, he nodded.

Glancing to the ceiling for inspiration and patience, I took a couple of quick breaths. "Elizabeth," I called clearly, realizing too late that I had just told my young son to be quiet.

Almost instantly, her pink door creaked open and she stood staring at me with an innocent smile. "Yes, Mom," she beamed. Her sandy hair, with roots that were turning the same warm hazel color of my own, was already scooped into a neat ponytail and she was dressed for school.

"Did you do this?" I asked her, holding up the bear that Dylan had named Frank.

She paused for a moment, perhaps resisting a child's knee-jerk compulsion to lie. "Well..." she mumbled, the smile slipping from her face and her almond eyes no longer able to meet mine.

"I'll take that as a 'yes'," I finished for her, moving to her door and placing my hand firmly around her wrist.

"It wasn't all my fault," she insisted, trying to snatch her hand back. "He started it!"

Rolling my eyes, my face moved back to Dylan who was suddenly also looking as guilty as sin. "What did you do to her?" I demanded, my patience wearing very thin.

"He pulled the head off Barbie," Lizzie whined.

My first instinct was to smile. Barbie had been a bone of contention. I hadn't wanted Lizzie to have one. In my opinion, Barbie promoted an unhealthy and unattainable body image, not to mention the distinctly materialistic and shallow nature of her 'lifestyle'. When Paul's parents learned of my disapproval, they promptly bought Lizzie a Barbie, complete with dream house, for Christmas. Her beheading didn't stress me in the slightest, but in the interests of being fair to the kids, I had to treat both crimes equally. So, I quickly quashed the tiny grin that played at the corners of my mouth.

"Dylan," I said firmly, crooking my finger at him in a 'come here' motion. Once I had the pair of them in front of me, I couched before them both. "I don't want to tell either of you this again," I began. "Dylan, you leave your sister's things alone, do you understand?"

I waited patiently for him to reluctantly nod. "Yes, Mommy," he mumbled, softly.

"And Lizzie," I added. "If your brother does something to upset you, don't retaliate, just come and tell me or your dad and we'll deal with it, okay?"

She was less willing to agree, but eventually did so. "Yes, Mom."

"I want you to apologize to each other," I concluded, wrapping my hand around my four-year-old son's waist and turning him to face his older sister.

"But Mom, I didn't-" Lizzie began.

I interrupted her with a lift of my index finger. "I don't want to hear any more about it, Elizabeth," I warned her. "You both did something wrong and I'm not in the mood to play who did something worse. Just apologize," I urged.

The pair mumbled a 'sorry' to each other and almost instantly turned their backs. With no energy to demand that they repeat it sincerely, I pushed myself back to my feet. "I'll get you some breakfast," I told them, making my way down the hall. When I reached the top of the stairs, I snapped my head back. "Oh and Lizzie, find Frank's arm. I'll try to reattach it."

"What about Barbie?" she quickly countered.

"I'll see what I can do," I promised with a wink. "But I don't know whether she'll pull through," I warned gravely.

She giggled, before rushing back into her room to find the various body parts.

It was an hour and a half before Paul made his way downstairs, and I was in the middle of clearing away the kids' plates and bowls. All three of them sat at the breakfast counter, Dylan swinging his legs wildly, with jelly all over his face; Lizzie studying a book; and little Kate strapped into her booster seat.

"Daddy," Dylan squealed, jumping down from his stool and sprinting across the tiles. He leaped into Paul's waiting arms and laughed hysterically as he was spun around rapidly.

"Hey champ," Paul smiled, setting our son back down before ruffling his hair. "You got a busy day ahead?" he asked. Dressed in a fresh suit, his open necked shirt neatly tucked into his dress pants, hair washed and combed, he looked very different from the way I'd left him on our bed.

"Very," our little boy confirmed with a nod. "I've got a meeting at eleven," he announced, clinging to his father's right leg as Paul heaved his way across the floor.

"Is that so?" Paul mumbled, only half listening, as he bent to kiss Kate on the top of the head. "Morning Liz," he added, looping an arm around her shoulders. "You okay, kiddo?"

She ignored his question in favor of one of her own. "Dad why do you have to go away again?"

"Sorry sweetie," he stated, with a tough luck tilt of his chin. "It's just the way it is, Daddy's a very busy man."

"But we never get to spend any time with you," she whined.

With a huff, Paul reached for a slice of bread and slipped it into the toaster. "We'll spend some time together when I get back, how's that?" he suggested.

Not even slightly appeased, Lizzie sullenly slipped down from her chair. "I've got to get ready for school," she muttered.

The Escort Next Door

"Daddy," Kate called, grinning. "Look," she proudly cried, holding up a crayon sketch that she'd been working on.

"That's great, honey," he responded, almost automatically, giving no more than a passing glance at the picture.

Somehow, knowing that the children were slipping from his radar of importance made me even more angry than the fact our relationship had taken a sideline. "Paul," I whispered, taking a step to his side. "You know, the kids really miss you when you're gone. It's tough on them; a few days for you feels like an eternity to them."

"I'll make it up to them," he shrugged, as his toast popped up and he quickly grabbed it. "I better toss some stuff in a bag," he announced, lifting his wrist to check the time.

Slipping my hand into the crook of his elbow, I held him still for just a few seconds longer. "I was hoping we'd be able to talk before you go," I suggested quietly and with no small degree of discomfort. It wasn't going to be an easy conversation to have.

"What about?" he replied testily, as he tugged his arm free of me.

"Well..." I hesitated, sure that he must know what I was referring to. "Last night," I eventually said in a whisper.

With an impatient sigh, his eyes drifted to the floor. "Do we have to do this now?" he asked.

"If not now, then when?" I countered.

Paul's gaze moved to Kate, who had gone back to adding more detail to her drawing, then Dylan, who was tearing about the open plan dining area as if he were an airplane. "Look," he said under his breath. "I was a little selfish," he admitted, but shrugged it off. "But you were the one complaining about how long it's been since we had sex. Well, we had sex, so...?" he left his words hanging, challenging me to make a big deal out of it.

If I'd been able to wrap my head around what was happening, I would have made a big deal out of it. But as things were, I stood open-mouthed, stunned into silence by his complete disregard for what had happened.

"So, are we done?" he demanded. "Because I've got a plane to catch." Without waiting for me to respond, he was already heading for the door.

Dylan ran after him yelling, "Can I come too, Dad?"

And sure enough, that was the end of it. We didn't speak of that night again.

Paul was ready by the time his driver arrived at the door. He handed over his small suitcase, before turning to hug and kiss each of the kids goodbye.

Once he was done, I received a wave of his hand as he climbed into the back of the vehicle.

After he'd gone, I still felt shell shocked by the callous way he'd rebuffed my concerns; both over the effect his repeated absences were having on the children, and indeed the trouble within our own strained relationship. And just when I thought the day couldn't possible have started any worse, his mother arrived. As she was apt to do, she didn't ring the bell, just let herself in. Paul had insisted she have a key, in case of emergencies, but Carole seemed to believe that gave her carte blanche to enter at will.

She strolled into the kitchen, finding me still in the midst of clearing up from breakfast. Lizzie and Dylan were arguing again, something I was too tried to deal with at that moment and unbeknownst to me, Kate had stripped off all of her clothes with the exception of her underwear.

The sight that met my mother-in-law caused her to tut loudly. "Having trouble, dear?" she asked rhetorically.

"Not exactly," I responded defensively. "They've just got me outnumbered at the moment," I added, smiling in an effort to lighten the mood.

It didn't work; it had never worked. I no longer knew why I bothered. Carole Hayes had hated me with a passion almost from the moment she met me.

She had it fixed in her head that I only wanted to be with her son because he was wealthy. Even agreeing to sign a rigid prenup that ensured I got nearly nothing if we divorced was not enough to convince her otherwise.

She was the kind of woman who made a sport of finding fault with other people; her favorite target being me. I wasn't good enough for her son, never had been, never would be. And she was determined to prove it to him.

"Well," she replied humorlessly. "I thought I might help you out by taking Elizabeth and Dylan to school."

"Umm, thanks," I said, busily loading the dishwasher.

"Do you want me to dress Katherine before I go?" she asked, turning to me with a disapprovingly arched eyebrow.

Driven to the point of caring minimally what she thought of me, I shrugged. "It's no problem," I said. "It's warm out. I'm in the middle of potty training her anyway, so it makes things simpler for her if she needs to go."

Scowling at me, she bit a tongue that no doubt had a stream of things to say on the matter. Rapidly she turned to the two older children, quickly breaking

The Escort Next Door

up their squabble. "Hey, grandma's here," she announced.

Dylan quickly ran to her, knowing, as I did, that she would have some treat for him. Sure enough, out of her Louis Vuitton purse came a sucker.

"Can I have this now, Mom?" he excitedly screamed, gratefully grabbing the candy.

"I don't-" I began.

"Of course you can," she interrupted.

My rule was always no sweets before school. "He's just brushed his teeth," I sighed, addressing Carole.

"He's a young boy," she smiled, relishing every opportunity she had to undermine me. "You've got to bend the rules and have a little fun now and then." As she spoke, her hand delved back into her purse and she retrieved another piece of candy. This time, she offered it to Lizzie.

"Thanks, grandma," Lizzie smiled, accepting the sucker and stuffing it into the pocket of her jeans.

"You can have yours now, too," Carole assured her, nodding.

"I'll save it for later, thanks," Lizzie replied.

This seemed to rankle my mother-in-law, who quickly said goodbye and hustled the older kids out of the house.

I followed them to the door, giving Lizzie and Dylan a hug. "Have a good day at school," I told them, before watching them trot down the steps and climb eagerly into the back of Grandma's Mercedes.

With just me and Kate in the house, things were much quieter. However, with a mountain of housework to do, they weren't going to be much easier.

Chapter Four

WHAT A MESS

Later that night, after an hour and a half and three stories, Kate finally went to sleep. At last, the house was silent and I breathed a sigh of relief. There was laundry to be done and dishes from dinner still to be washed, but I couldn't be bothered with either. Instead, I plodded wearily to my bathroom and ran a nice, hot bath.

I couldn't contain the long, deep sigh I exhaled as my body slipped beneath the warm water and it seemed as if a huge weight had been lifted from me. Under the spell of that glorious calm, my brain stopped whirring and, for the first time in longer than I cared to recall, I was at peace.

I made no conscious decision to move my hands. In fact, I surprised myself when I found them slipping over the slick skin of my chest and caressing my breasts. Quickly giving way to the pleasant sensation, I allowed my eyes to lazily drift closed, as I continued to move my fingers in slow, teasing circles. When I reached my nipples, I found them rigid and aching. Gently gripping those tight pebbles between my forefingers and thumbs, I pinched lightly. "Hmmm," I mumbled longingly, my right hand leaving my breasts and smoothing over my abdomen.

With my eyes shut, I imagined another hand traveling to my navel and slowly sliding over my mound. It was Paul I thought about. It had always been Paul; except perhaps for a short time when I was sixteen, when mind candy for my self-exploration was the blonde-haired guy from that boy band. The fact that Paul was, and always had been, the focus of almost all of my erotic fantasies wasn't due to any misplaced sense of disloyalty via thought. It was simply a case of never having felt the need to focus on any other man. My husband turned me on – not everything about him, of course. The sight of him sprawled out on the bed that morning, for example, was not the stuff of my sexual dreams. However, there were always memories that I could hang my masturbating hat on. We'd had some really good times together, and it wasn't difficult for me to focus on those.

My fingers moved leisurely over the neat triangle of short hair that covered my mound. Drawn further, they smoothed between my outer lips finding them smooth and plump. Bending one leg and sliding my foot up to my bottom, I offered my own roaming hand freer access. With the pad of my middle finger, I rolled carefully over my clitoris, which instantly responded.

Often, during moments like those, I'd think of the first time Paul touched me like that. It was several months before we went the whole way and not long after my eighteenth birthday. He'd been so nervous that his fingers were trembling. He didn't know what he was doing, and truth be told, neither did I. Sure, I knew what felt good, but I hadn't got a name for that small bud that sent warmth flooding through my entire body. We were both giddy and a little scared, but we laughed together and, eventually, he asked me to guide his fingers.

"Show me," he'd urged. "Show me how to touch you."

I was hesitant at first, sure that he'd much rather be in control of the situation. I was also reluctant to give the impression that he was doing something wrong. However, he continued to insist and, as I placed my fingers on top of his, it wasn't close to being as embarrassing or awkward as I'd assumed it would be. That afternoon, I'd coaxed him into rubbing my clitoris, until I bucked and writhed in climax. What I didn't know then, and would never have known had he not confessed it a couple of years later, was that the sight and feel of my orgasm had caused Paul to come in his pants.

Brought back to my present surroundings by the stirring of electricity between my legs, I started to increase the pressure of my touch. It had been several weeks since I'd pleasured myself and even longer since Paul had driven me to orgasm, so the speed of its climb caught me off guard. Usually, after long dry spells, my body is slow to reach boiling point.

I was close; so close. My mouth fell open and I began suck in shallow panted breaths. My hips were moving of their own volition, my backside swaying on the bottom of the tub in rhythm to the movement of my fingers. Sparks were triggering a restless warmth in my belly. And then, as I began to reach the summit, the phone's harsh ringing ripped me from the high and yanked me back down. I tried to ignore it, I kept my eyes tightly shut and strummed my body with renewed vigor. However, as the beep of the answer machine cut in and my mother-in-law's voice drifted to the bathroom from the phone on Paul's

The Escort Next Door

bedside table, I removed my hand from between my legs with a muttered, "Shit."

"Julia, it's Carole," she began in her hash, nasal tone. "I just wanted to make sure everything's okay. I know you said you can cope, but I really think that things are becoming too much for you right now. It's understandable," she quickly added. "It's hard for an inexperienced mother to care for three children on her own."

The bath was suddenly no longer relaxing. My jaw had tightened and I felt my shoulders begin to rise to my neck. What she meant by 'inexperienced mother' I didn't know. I'd been a mom for nearly eight years and certainly didn't consider myself new to the job.

"All I mean is, there's nothing wrong with asking for help. And I'm always here if you need me," she announced, a smile clear in her voice. "Anyway," she added briskly. "Call me, because it's really quite late and I'm concerned about where you are."

"Argh," I growled, my hands gripping the edges of the bathtub and imagined it was her neck beneath my fingers. With the firm click of her phone being put down, I gave up all hope of a soothing soak in the tub, let alone any prospect of sexual release. Yanking myself up, I reached for a big, fluffy towel with one hand and held it loosely to my chest, not bothering to wrap it around me. After quickly tugging the plug out of the bath, I wandered bare foot and dripping into the bedroom.

Once there, I stared at the phone, with a red light blinking on its base, for several seconds. Should I call her? If I did, she'd jabber on and on for ages. If I didn't, she'd just keeping calling all night long. Making a sudden decision, I lunged forwards and edged the bedside table out slightly. Then, I grabbed the cable at the back of the phone and pulled until I felt the mains pop out of the wall socket.

With a satisfied nod and a naughty grin, I flopped down onto the bed. Knowing exactly what Carole would think if she could see me making the bed wet with the outline of my buttocks, I dropped onto my back. Sprawling out, I let my soaking wet hair drench the sheets. However, my delight in doing something that seemed so rebellious was short-lived. Eventually, I sat up and, when I did, I was met with my first real acknowledgment of the car crash that was my bedroom.

Up until that time, I hadn't been back in the room since leaving it that morning. And as I'd strolled to the bath, I'd failed to really take it in. Carole's opinion that I was a lazy wife and mother came back to haunt me. Our bedroom certainly was a mess, not of my making but, apparently, it was my 'job' to clean up after my husband.

There were clothes everywhere. The ones Paul had worn the night before were strewn on the floor from where he'd stripped them off that morning. His damp towel had been tossed at the foot of the bed and now just a tiny corner clung to the mattress while the rest draped slovenly on the floor. A sports bag sat beside the wardrobe. It was open with a creased shirt spilling out of it. This was the bag he'd taken on his last trip and must have been placed in the closet when he got home. Paul appeared to have pulled it out and been rummaging for something. Thoughtfully, he'd left it in disarray for me to deal with.

I considered leaving it; just watching TV and putting all that mess off until the morning. However, I couldn't take my eyes off the state of the room and was bombarded by the thought that I wasn't being a good enough wife to Paul. I was supposed to *want* to take care of him, it wasn't meant to seem like a chore. Perhaps he felt, like his mom, that I wasn't doing a very good job – was that why we'd been so disconnected?

Pushing myself up from the bed, I quickly strode back into the bathroom, tossed the towel in the laundry hamper and grabbed a robe. It was a silk one that reached my calves; a present from Paul for my birthday. Carefully drawing the tie around my middle and securing it in place, I didn't care that my damp hair was already soaking through the material at my shoulders.

Marching back into the bedroom, I pushed the sleeves of the robe up to my elbows and was ready for business. I moved quickly around the room, first picking up Paul's towel and scooping that over my arm as I bent for his clothes. While I walked purposefully to the large bathroom hamper, I slipped my hands into his pants pockets, turning them inside out. True to form, a handful of change clattered onto the bathroom tiles.

"Paul," I groaned, realizing that after a decade of begging him, he was never going to empty the pockets of his dirty clothes.

After tossing my armful into the laundry basket, I crouched and picked up each coin one by one. Two quarters, three dimes and five pennies. With a huff of weariness, I pushed myself upright and took the fistful of money to Paul's bedside table. Right next to the phone was a sterling silver tray with 'change is good' engraved in the center. It had once belonged to Paul's grandfather and, although he treasured it, he didn't see fit to use it. With a satisfying clatter, I placed the coins onto the tray and spun on the balls of my feet.

The Escort Next Door

The sports bag was the one remaining eyesore. I would have felt that I was on the home stretch, but the worst thing about being a housewife is that there's never a home stretch. There's always something to do; always more mess, because while you're cleaning someone's making some more. But, for the time being at least, I was on the verge of having a clean bedroom.

I moved for the bag, gripping the thick shoulder strap and half lifted, half dragged it into the bathroom. Setting it down by the still open hamper, I crouched down and began tugging each item of clothing from the bag. Two dress shirts went straight into the basket. A white T-shirt followed and then there were three boxer shorts. Black dress pants and a pair of jeans dwelt at the bottom and, sure enough, both had change and receipts stuffed in every available pocket.

"For God's sake," I muttered pulling out all the junk and chucking it temporarily in the bottom of the bag. As I did that, my eyes flashed down at the black polyester lining that was speckled with tiny balls of white fluff. My gaze caught something shiny. Releasing their grip on Paul's jeans, my fingers delved into the bag. I tried to tell myself that it was just a little scrap of foil; it couldn't possibly be what it looked like; what I thought it was. Grasping it with my forefinger and thumb, I slowly pulled it free from its hiding place. It wasn't just the tiny edge I had been able to see. It was a full square with a clear circular indent. The shiny, blue wrapper had been ripped at the top and its contents removed.

The hand holding the condom wrapper began to tremble, as the implications of it settled painfully in my chest. My mouth and throat went instantly dry, while palpitations caused my eardrums to throb with each deep, pound of my heart. Paul and I hadn't used condoms since our engagement; he'd never liked them, we both wanted a family anyway and, shortly after Lizzie was born, I'd started taking the pill. There was no need for any other form of contraception.

The object in my hand could mean only one thing. God knows I tried to find other explanations. Most of them were wild, nonsensical excuses; anything to avoid the truth that was staring me in the face. But there was no way to avoid it. Paul had an affair while he'd been away.

Dropping the wrapper and swiveling toward the tub, bile suddenly rose in my throat. I dry heaved, nothing more than saliva dribbling from my bottom lip while my throat burned. I remained that way for several minutes, my empty stomach continuing to retch.

Eventually, my insides stopped trying to turn themselves inside out, but my heart still raced and my fingers tingled with a lack of circulation. My knees beginning to feel numb, I forced myself up, regretting it almost instantly when my head pounded and I felt a wave of dizziness. Nevertheless, I pulled myself around to the sink and turned the cold faucet on full. I let the stream flow noisily for a second, while I looked at myself in the mirror. My usually bright complexion was deathly pale and my blue eyes gazed blankly ahead. Unable to bear the sight of myself, I stuck my head beneath the water's stream, vigorously rinsing my face before filling my mouth with several large gulps.

When the feeling of nausea returned with a vengeance, I quickly turned off the water and slipped down onto the cold tiles, my legs collapsing beneath me. My back propped up against the edge of the tub was the only thing keeping me sitting upright. Never, either before or since, have I experienced such a sudden and debilitating sense of loss and disorientation.

It was an hour or more before I was finally able to drag myself up from the bathroom floor. By that point, I was still trembling, but it was no longer with fear. The victim mentality had been replaced with anger; a seething rage. Questions swirled around my frenzied brain, and I was determined to get answers.

Chapter Five

Proof

Through an enraged red mist, I wasn't thinking clearly. I flew back into the bedroom and started tearing the room apart. I began by ripping out the drawers of Paul's bedside table, and tipping the contents of them on the floor. His collection of cufflinks scattered over the carpet and an old cell phone battery clunked to the ground followed by an ipod with tangled earphones. The lower, deeper drawer was heavier and full of notebooks and photo albums. I flicked through these, quickly dismissing them when I found nothing relevant within the pages.

Using the bed to push myself up, I moved over to Paul's wardrobe. My movements were frenzied, as I tugged suit jackets off hangers and rifled through the pockets. When I found nothing, I tossed the clothes over my shoulder. I continued this way, until I'd gone through every item of clothing he owned. I had to wade through an ankle deep puddle of fabric as I turned away from the closet and glanced desperately around the room. He had taken everything else with him; his phone, tablet and laptop were all in his possession.

"Shit," I hissed, my breath coming hard as the desperate need to get to the truth became an almost physical pain. I couldn't call him, he'd only come up with a convenient excuse for the condom, and not being able to see him when he lied put me at a disadvantage. No, I wanted to have irrefutable proof of what he'd done before I confronted him with it.

In the corner of the room was a desktop computer, which I focused on intently. It was my only route into his life. I'd only ever used the thing infrequently, but I'd worked with computers before Lizzie came into the world, and knew my way around them. Without a second thought, I turned it on and tugged the antique chair toward the desk.

Sitting, I grasped the mouse and clicked on the shortcut for Paul's email. Then, I was forced to pause. I had no idea what his password was. It wasn't something he'd shared with me. Until that moment, I'd never questioned it; hadn't believed for one second that I needed access to his cell or his computers. I'd stupidly believed that Paul loved me the same way I loved him, and that no matter what problems we faced, we'd work through them together.

Not only did I feel betrayed and sick with the knowledge that he'd been with someone else, but I also felt stupid. I was gullible and naïve not to see what had been going on. The signs were there; his distance, his unwillingness to have sex (the exception being our strange encounter the night before), that gnawing sense that something just wasn't right. It was a feeling I'd had for weeks, and yet I'd ignored it, buried it, pretended that everything was just peachy and perfect.

With no trace of humor, I laughed bitterly at my own stupidity.

Fresh anger welling inside me, I turned my attention back to the computer screen. I began typing words that floated into my head. I started with the name of Paul's family business: 'Hayes&Son', then moved onto the license plate number of his new BMW, the name of his childhood dog, our children's names and dates of birth, the date of our wedding. Denied, denied, denied.

"Argh," I groaned loudly, slamming my hand down on the surface of the desk. In the silence that followed, I waited to discover that I'd woken one, or possibly all three, of the kids. However, the moment's ticked by and still silence met my ears. Drawing in a calming breath, I resolved to control my outburst. The last thing I needed was a sleepily toddler wandering in and asking what was going on. I would never be able to explain Mom's teary, haunted face or the wreckage she'd made of the bedroom.

With a sigh of resignation, I threw myself back into the solid wooden-backed chair, jarring my spine as I did so. I didn't care about the discomfort. Instead, my eyes crawled up the wall before me and landed on a framed picture of Paul with three of his high school football teammates. "Tigers," I whispered under my breath.

Moving without my conscious request, I typed, 'Tigers' into the empty password box. However, I hovered over the enter key for some time, before deciding to add '32', Paul's jersey number. The screen suddenly changed and I was looking at Paul's inbox.

Quickly scanning through the first page of recent messages, all seemed normal, boring and business-like. However, three quarters of the way down the page, I noticed something that seemed out of place. The sender's name was Jennifer, in of itself nothing to be suspicious about, but the subject line of her email read, 'Last Night'.

Terrified, but unable to simply turn away, I slowly directed the mouse to that message and clicked to open it. I don't think I breathed as I read, and my heart seemed to sink lower and lower in my chest.

Hi Paul,
Just wanted to say thanks for a very interesting evening. Someone told me that you admire people who go after what they want, so I assume you won't think any less of me for doing exactly that. Like I told you, I'd been thinking about it for months and the temptation of being in a strange city and a luxurious hotel with you was just too great to resist. And I think you should know that you definitely didn't disappoint! Anyway, I look forward to working with you. I'm pretty sure it's going to be a lot of fun for both of us.

There was nothing overt, but the subtext of her email left little to the imagination. My eyes flicked to the date, it had been sent almost three months ago. Paul had been on another three, maybe four trips since then. The tears that had been pricking my eyes spilled silently onto my cheek and traced a hot trail to my chin. This hadn't just been a one-time thing; a moment of weakness. In all likelihood, he'd been having a full-blown affair with this woman.

Desperate to know more, I typed Jennifer in the search box and pulled up all messages sent to and from her. There were only two more that she'd sent to Paul, both were completely professional and written some time earlier. The other was written by Paul in reply to the first email I'd read.

Jen,

The pleasure was mine! You're absolutely right, this could be the start of a long and successful association. Will be in Dallas again in a couple of weeks. If interested in another meeting, let me know. I'll e-mail you the details when they're set in stone.

Again, the pretext of business hid something that caused my stomach to lurch. Blinking back the water that was blurring my vision, I slumped in the chair. There were still so many unanswered questions. Who was this woman? How long had it been going on? Was it just a fling or was Paul considering leaving me for her?

It seemed as though I'd struck a dead end. Paul and this Jennifer hadn't corresponded in ten weeks, at least not via email. However, as I was about to give up, I noticed that Paul had placed those two emails, which seemed to skirt around the subject of a night spent together, in a folder entitled, 'business trips'. I'm not sure why it occurred to me to check it, but I did so on instinct.

Moving the mouse to the right hand side of the screen, I clicked on the folder, which opened a new window. 'Business trips' contained dozens of messages and as I scanned down the list, I quickly noticed the pattern. Every single one was from a woman. Four names featured heavily; Abby, Rachel, Joann and Krista. Emails from each of them were predominantly in dated chunks. Abby's were all sent just before and around the time Paul was in New York. Rachel's centered around the week he was in Tampa. Joann wrote to him during his trip to San Francisco, and Krista's emails were dated on and just after Paul's visit to San Diego.

"Jesus," I mumbled, my eyes widening with disbelief. It all seemed so surreal. Shaking my head, I felt that I must be dreaming. This had to be some horrible nightmare that I was about to wake up from. However, no matter how many times I blinked, the image on the screen stayed the same.

Although a part of me didn't want the pain of knowing what was inside those emails, the urge to get to the truth was overwhelming. So, regardless of the sensible voice that told me to just turn the computer off and walk away, my fingers gripped the mouse tightly and directed the cursor to the last email on the list – the oldest. It was from Krista and the subject line read, 'Discrete'.

Paul,
I'm sure you feel the same, but I wanted to ask if we can keep what happened yesterday between us. Some of the guys on my team were asking where I disappeared to last

night and I made up an excuse about not feeling well. I just hope nobody saw us going upstairs to your room. I don't want people thinking that I'm trying to sleep my way to a promotion. Working with a large group of men is difficult enough without them thinking I'm a slut. And as drunk as we both were, I don't want you to think I regret what happened. In fact, if you're in town for a few more days, perhaps we can meet up again?

Her next message made it clear that Paul had reassured her and responded in the affirmative to her final question. She simply confirmed that she would meet him at his hotel room at 9pm that evening.

There followed a couple more messages, stating that she'd had a good time and requested more meetings with him. The content of her final email suggested that Paul had given her the brush off. However, she didn't seem too distressed by that news.

Next came Joann, her messages were similar in tone. She obviously also worked for the company, in one of the smaller branches. She alluded to having given Paul a blowjob in the bathroom of a restaurant, before signing off with a crass remark about her jaw still being sore from the experience.

With a disgusted grunt, I shut that email and opened the next. It was immediately apparent that

The Escort Next Door

Rachel from Tampa was direct in expressing her desires.

Mr. Hayes,
This is probably totally inappropriate, but I know you're here for the weekend and I was hoping you might like a little company. I feel that there's been some chemistry between us and I've caught you glancing at me in a way that tells me you've felt it too. I know that you're married, and I'm not looking for anything serious. I just want you to fuck me.

There were several very short messages, confirming a time and place to meet. Then, a day later, a long message praising Paul's prowess. However, she, unlike the two other women, seemed content with just one night. She made no mention of meeting him again, and continued to address him as Mr. Hayes.

The final clutch of emails was the most recent, concerning Paul's trip to New York. There, he'd been supposed to be meeting with potential new clients. The Abby from his mailbox seemed to be an employee of that business.

Hello, Paul.
I'm Abby, Frank Welby's personal assistant. I tried to call you this afternoon, but couldn't get through. Mr. Welby was impressed with your presentation, but he'd like some further questions answered before you leave town. However, he's heading to Napa tomorrow, so would it be possible

for you to get down to the offices tonight? Thanks in advance.

I read this message again, searching for some innuendo or hint of over familiarity that I might have missed the first time around. There was none, so why had Paul kept this message? The fact that there was another email from Abby indicated there was more to this seemingly professional exchange. With a sense of dread, I clicked on the subsequent message.
Paul,

I forgot that there was a security camera in the conference room! Had to do some quick thinking to remove this footage from the files. I really enjoyed watching this, though. Hope you will, too.

Beneath the text was a video file. In so deep, I felt sure things could get no worse. I was wrong.

A new window quickly opened and a grainy image appeared. The picture was soundless and quality awful, but there was no mistaking my husband. He was standing behind a blonde-haired woman, with her shoulder length hair masking most of her face. She was bent forward over a massive circular table with some ten chairs around it. Her large breasts were threatening to spill out of the low cut blouse she wore.

Paul had her tight, very short skirt tugged into his hands and yanked up around her waist. I then watched his left hand, the one bearing his solid gold wedding band, slide down to his pants and unzip his fly. His fingers disappeared within and quickly returned, easing his hard shaft through the opening. Suddenly, he was inside her. With no thought for contraception, he'd rammed his unprotected member into a woman he'd met just that morning. The knowledge that less than a week later, that same cock was inside me made me feel that I'd been defiled.

Her head bucked up and she arched her back, her mouth open as she screamed something. Paul instantly took advantage of her elevated upper half, grasping both of her breasts in rough hands. After a few seconds of frenzied groping, she turned her face to his and said something I couldn't lipread. It spurred him into action, pushing her back to the desk and slamming his erection into her with a force that rocked the huge table.

All of the blood left my head, as I watched him repeatedly enter her from behind. She was writhing beneath him, squealing in what looked like delight at the violent treatment. Paul abruptly pulled free from her, using his right hand to slap her hard on the buttock before clasping his penis. With hurried, brutal strokes, he stimulated himself. Climaxing with a sudden jet of creamy white fluid that splattered over the hand print that was reddening on her ass.

Jumping to my feet, I dashed to the bathroom, making it to the sink just in time to lose the small amount of water I'd managed to force into my stomach just minutes before.

Chapter Six

WHAT FRIENDS ARE FOR

Unable to think clearly, I dashed back into the bedroom and flung open my closet. Yanking out a suitcase that was laid on the bottom, I flipped it open and began throwing clothes into it. I couldn't say what I chose to take and what I chose to leave, there was no logical sense to what I was doing, no thought for practicalities. The only thing I was aware of was a desperate need to get out of that house. A claustrophobia had gripped me and was frantic to break free.

Enclosing the hurriedly bundled clothes within the case, I grabbed a pair of sweatpants with my free hand. Rushing to the bed, I sat down and slipped the sweats over my legs. Keeping the robe fastened and draped over the top, I pulled the pants up to my waist and jumped up from the mattress. It was only as I returned to my closet and grasped an oversized sweater that I silently asked, what was I doing? Where would I go? I didn't have any money, no family nearby and, after I'd left Paul, he was sure to do everything he could to take the children away from me. He could afford a team of the best family law attorneys. I could afford...nothing.

As all the furious energy drained from me, I slumped to the floor of my closet and leaned back against the firm wall. I was trapped.

Staring blankly ahead, I wrestled with that concept; questioning how I'd found myself in such a situation. It had never entered my head, not even for a second, that by agreeing to Paul's parents' demands over the prenuptial agreement, I'd been backed into an inescapable corner. The balance of power in our marriage was hideously weighted in his favor. And I was out of options.

In a state of utter despondency and still reeling from what I'd just discovered, I did what I have always done when I didn't know what to do. I picked up the phone, after plugging it back in, and called Grace. She was my best friend, had been since we were in second grade. Although life had sent us in different directions, quite literally placing us on opposite sides of the country, and things often got so busy that it would be months between conversations, we remained close. Every time we talked, even when it was almost a year since the last time, it was as though we'd just seen each other yesterday. We both understood that life got frantic, so there was no sense that the other wasn't making 'enough effort' to stay in touch.

Waiting anxiously for her to answer, I clutched the phone tightly to my ear as if it were a lifeline.

"Hello," she eventually said, a slight question in the word which made it obvious she hadn't looked at the caller ID before picking up.

"Hey," I replied, my voice sounding hoarse and scratchy. "It's me."

"Julia?" she responded quickly. "What's up? You sound terrible."

Despite the intense misery I felt, I couldn't help but smile. Grace always had a way of cutting right to the heart of the matter. She didn't worry about a veneer of politeness, she never said anything she didn't mean and expected everybody to treat her with the same level of brutal honesty.

"Jesus," she added. "It must be three in the morning there. What the hell's happened?"

"Is it?" I mumbled absently glancing at the digital clock. "I lost track of time."

"Jules," she sighed soothingly. "What's going on?"

"I umm," I began, not knowing exactly what to say. After a brief pause, I decided perhaps Grace's approach was the best, if not the only, way to deal with things. "Paul's been cheating on me."

"What?" she shouted, her shock sounding no less than my own had been.

I was past the point of crying, all of my tears had dried out long before. So, it was with a sort of detached, emotionless voice that I recounted what I'd discovered over the previous few hours.

"You've got to be kidding me?" she muttered quietly. I could tell she was talking to herself and didn't actually think it was my idea of a practical joke. "Who does that bastard think he is?"

"Rico Suave, apparently," I murmured bitterly.

"Jesus Christ," she sighed, clearly having a hard time taking the news in. "What an ass!" she suddenly shouted. "Where the fuck does he get off? You're stuck at home raising his children and he goes around sticking his dick into everything with a pair of breast."

I was grateful that she was so angry on my behalf, but her rant brought back images that caused my throat to tighten.

"I'd chop his cock off!" she added vehemently.

That brought a reluctant laugh to my lips, but it tapered off far too quickly to provide any real relief.

"Oh, Jules," she breathed. "Honey, what are you going to do?"

"I really don't know," I admitted with a whisper. "I just..." I sighed wearily. "I don't know."

"But you are going to leave him, right?" she asked, leaving no doubt that she felt the answer should be a resounding 'yes'.

"I want to," I replied weakly. "I mean, our marriage is over. If it had just been once, I might have been able to forgive him, but after this, I'll never be able to trust him again."

"But?" Grace coaxed, noting that there was one coming.

"But what can I do?" I said, shaking my head dispiritedly. "I haven't got a penny to my name. I can't even afford to rent a tiny one bedroom apartment, let alone a place big enough for three kids."

"Okay," she conceded, her practical tone coming to the fore. "So, you get a job and save some money."

It was a viable suggestion, but there were problems. "I won't be able to work without Paul finding out," I sighed. "He'd want to know why, and I can't come up with a convincing reason other than the truth."

"Tell him you're bored at home and need some adult company once in a while," Grace offered helpfully.

"Yeah," I agreed. "But if he knows I'm working, he'll wonder why the money isn't going into our joint bills account," I countered, hating the fact that every solution simply posed another problem. "Not to mention the fact that it would take me forever to save enough, I'm not qualified for anything that would pay well."

"Then don't worry about money," she dismissed quickly. "You and the children can come and live with me, until you've got yourself settled financially. You could stay as long as it takes you know that."

I'd been wrong. My tears had apparently an endless supply, because Grace's generous offer brought a fresh wave. "You're too good to me," I replied shakily.

"Hey," she cooed. "That's what friends are for, right? So what do you say?"

"I'd love to," I told her earnestly. "But I can't. No matter what, when I leave him, Paul's going to fight me for principal custody of the kids. If I take them out of the state without his permission, his lawyers will make sure I never see them again."

Grace was silent for several seconds. "Surely, he wouldn't do that," she mumbled. "The children love you, you're a good mom. Why would he want to do that to them or to you?"

Sighing, my eyes wandered to the ceiling. "He can be very vindictive," I explained. "And he's ruthless in getting what he wants. He's, umm..." I hesitated. "He's joked about what would happen if we ever split up. At least, he framed them as jokes, but I knew that he wasn't just messing around. If I give him any reason to, he'll take them from me."

Exhaling heavily, the whir of Grace's brain almost came through the phone. "All right," she began. "So, the situation is you need to make some money, preferably a lot of it in a fairly short space of time. And you need to keep it on the down low," she stated, summing up my impossible situation.

"That's about it," I agreed, leaning forward and dropping my head into my open left palm. "No big deal, right?" I joked darkly.

"Well," she said, drawing the word out. "I'm thinking there is something you could do?"

"What?" I asked, not holding out much hope for a completely full proof solution.

"Don't dismiss it right off the bat, okay?" she prefaced. "How about working as an exotic dancer?"

"Stripping?" I blurted. "I don't think so."

"I said, don't dismiss it," she insisted. "Think about it. You could work a couple of nights a week during the time Paul's away. You'd hire a sitter to watch the kids, or have them stay overnight with friends."

"All that sounds fine," I conceded. "But what about the part where I take off my clothes?"

"You've got an amazing body," she instantly replied, seeming to misunderstand my main objection. "It may have been a long time since you danced in high school, but I bet you've still got the moves."

"Grace," I muttered. "I can't."

"Why not?" she countered.

"I just..." I weakly protested. "I can't go around all the clubs in town, gyrating in nothing more than a thong."

"You could," she retorted. "Do you know how quickly you could make enough money for a deposit on an apartment?"

"That's not the point," I replied quietly.

"Well, sweetie," she sighed. "I don't know that you have many other options. I'm not suggesting that it's perfect, and I'm not suggesting you take it up as a career. But I do think it's worth considering. Otherwise, what choice do you have?" We both knew it was a rhetorical question, but Grace left it hanging there, no doubt wanting to ensure that I really thought about my predicament and lack of ways out. "Do you really think that you could just bury all of this and go on with Paul as though nothing's happened?" she eventually added.

That was another question that didn't require an answer. She knew me well enough to know that I couldn't bear to play 'happy families' with a man who not only had been unfaithful, but also a man who would doubtless continue to cheat on me.

"Are you still there?" she said after my silence had become uncomfortably long.

"Yeah," I assured her quietly. "Yeah, I'm still here. I'm just wondering how I got myself into this mess."

"None of this is your fault," she replied softly. "You could never have known that this is what was going to happen. I mean," she added, "it's not as though Paul was a player when he was younger. He's changed, and you couldn't have foreseen that."

"Maybe," I reluctantly mumbled. "But he still changed right in front of me, and I was either too busy or too blind to notice."

"Jules," she said in her no nonsense manner. It was the kind of tone that all parents use with their children from time to time. "You have to stop beating yourself up. Paul is the one who did something wrong. You're not to blame for any of it, understand?"

"I guess," I replied halfheartedly.

"Listen, I'm really sorry, but I've got to go," she added apologetically. I could hear Mason, her baby boy, in the background. He was crying softly; the sound of a hungry, growing child. "Think about what I said, and call me again if you need to talk. Any time, day or night."

"Thank you," I said with a grateful half smile that she would never see, but I hope she heard. "I really appreciate that."

"No problem," she responded. "You take care, honey."

"Bye," I sadly whispered, before slipping the phone back into its base. My gaze stayed fixed there for some time, not because I was drawn to the phone in particular. No, my focus remained there, because I was trying to resist the call of something else. If I ignored it, perhaps the feeling would pass.

However, it didn't. Eventually, I peered over my shoulder at the computer. After all that time, the screen had gone blank and a small amber light blinking slowly in the right hand corner. It was insane, I told myself. There was no way I would dance for ten dollar bills to be tucked into my panties. So, it was pointless even looking. And yet, my curiosity remained. In fact, it began to grow.

Muttering, "This is ridiculous," I picked myself off the bed and settled back in the chair by the desk.

Quickly grabbing the mouse, I swept it across the pad, enlivening the screen once more. Not wishing to be reminded of the content of Paul's emails, I quickly signed out and closed that window. Then, I opened a fresh page and began a search.

After just a few minutes, I'd discovered that the pay of strippers varied dramatically depending on the clubs and how many private dances they were willing to offer. Nevertheless, it was apparently very possible for women to make between $2,000 and $3,000 per week. When I compared that with all of the entry level positions I would be qualified for, which paid minimum wage or just above, the choice seemed like a no-brainer. Grace was right, within just a few weeks, I could make enough money to put down a deposit and have a nice nest egg saved up.

Suddenly becoming aware of what I was doing, I pushed away from the desk and leaned back in the chair. "Am I actually considering this?" I whispered. I had shocked myself by how quickly I'd warmed to the idea and how attractive it was suddenly seeming.

Yes, it still seemed seedy. But I was beginning to realize I could live with that. After all, it would be for a finite, very short period of time. The alternative would mean staying with Paul, essentially prostituting myself (when he felt like having sex with me and not someone else), and trawling through a loveless, miserable existence. Being leered at by a few lonely men was a small price to pay to be free.

A silly smile began to spread across my face. There was another bonus to this plan, it would feel really good to get my own pay back on Paul. Although he'd never find out what I was doing, I could guess what his reaction would be if he did know. And that was enough; at least some vengeance would be had.

However, with that thought came an abrupt dampener to my heightening spirits. Paul could never know what I was doing. If he learned I was dancing in those places, despite the expression on his face being priceless, he would use it to argue that I was an unfit mother. If I danced in public, especially in the classier clubs that would be my preference, there was a possibility I'd be seen by someone Paul knows. That was a risk I could simply not afford to take.

Chapter Seven

Work

Over the next couple of days, I continued to think very seriously about the possibility of stripping. Every time I stepped out of the shower, I carefully examined my body. For a woman who'd had three children, I wasn't in bad shape. Regular exercise and being usually careful to avoid any kind of junk food, had helped me stay trim. There were a few silvery stretch marks around my hips, but they were barely noticeable. After prodding my butt, I discovered a little wobble, but it was still pretty firm. Most of my skin was healthily bronzed by the summer sun, and the problem of paler patches could be easily solved with a little spray tan.

With the help of more make-up than I'd usually wear and the right outfit, I didn't think I'd look out of place in one of the more upmarket clubs. The more I thought, the more I became convinced not only that I could do it, but that it also offered me the escape route I needed.

As my interest refused to wane, I went back onto the internet and began scouting for clubs in various cities around the state. I was surprised by the large number of so-called gentleman's clubs. Most of their websites offered a section for 'career opportunities' and stressed that they were always looking for new talent. One page provided potential customers with a gallery of their dancers. Out of curiosity, I browsed the girls noting that many of them linked to their own websites.

Clicking on a blonde named, 'Snow', I was intrigued as to why a stripper would need a website. It turned out, Snow was a savvy business woman. She worked in a number of clubs and also offered private services in both dancing and escorting. Not only was she gaining some job security by diversifying, but also making a lot more money. With one night of escorting, she was earning what the average stripper gets in a week.

Closing the browser, I thought no more about it. At least, I wasn't aware of thinking about it. But as I lay in bed that night, my eyes wide open and focused on shadows that played across the ceiling, I continued to think about Snow and what she chose to do for a living. Sure, it was prostitution, and yet it was a very different world to the streetwalking variety.

Two things quickly occurred to me. One, if I stayed with Paul, I was going to be prostituting myself anyway. And two, men who hire escorts are much more likely to be discreet than men who go to strip joints.

Shaking my head, I couldn't quite believe the conclusions I was reaching. But one after another, I kept producing reasons why a brief career as an escort would be a good idea. I'd only have to work one night per week; I wouldn't have to take my clothes off in front of a room full of people; I could be selective over my clients and where I met them, ensuring I was always out of town.

But, I quickly slammed on the breaks of my runaway train of thought, there was the one huge sacrifice I would need to make. I would need to be prepared to allow complete strangers to use my body for their sexual pleasure. Was that something I could do? Was it something I would be able to live with afterward? The truth was, I didn't know.

However, there were only two alternatives; continue with the sham that was my marriage or leave

Paul and accept that he would fight to take primary custody of our kids. I knew without any equivocation that I could live with neither of those things. The possible fallout may have been a complete unknown, but the fear of what *might* happen was far less than the dread of playing the dutiful wife to a man I no longer respected, trusted or loved.

Unable to close my eyes, I pushed the covers off the bed and sat up. "I can try," I mumbled beneath my breath. "Just once."

Slipping off the bed, I tiptoed in the darkness to the computer and once more turned it on. If I'd made up my mind, I told myself, then I might as well get the ball rolling.

I wouldn't be able to set up my own site, at least not one in which I used a photograph, as there was too much chance of Paul, his parents, our friends and God knew who else seeing it. Instead, I'd need to use classified ads. There were several sites that would allow me to post free ones and there were a couple of message boards that offered a forum for escorts and potential clients to communicate.

After having read several other ads, I began to get a gist for the basic format and the kind of things that were important to customers. It took me almost an hour to write my own pitch, it was only 100 words long, but I struggled with the tone, wanting to get the right balance between classy and alluring. It's difficult enough to sell yourself for a regular job, when you're quite literally selling yourself, a personal statement (even a very short one) becomes incredibly hard.

However, by the time dawn broke, I had advertised myself on a total of five websites and had set up a new email account for the purpose.

Given the sheer number of young women who seemed to be trying to get work in exactly the same way, I didn't hold out much hope of hearing from anyone in the near future. In fact, regardless of the large amounts of money that could be made, I was beginning to wonder whether I would be able to make anything at all. There seemed to be a disproportionately large supply compared with demand.

Deciding that I would give the ads a couple of weeks, I determined to worry about a 'Plan B' only after that time had elapsed.

In the meantime, I had to go back to being a mom; there were children that needed to be woken, fed and shipped off to school.

***

As it turned out, I didn't have to wait two weeks. Just three days passed before I received my first email inquiry. I'd almost dismissed it as spam, feeling sure that I had no chance of generating interest so quickly. However, the subject line, 'Looking for some company on Saturday night', caused me to stop dead in my tracks.

I was about to open the message, but a voice from the doorway caused me to jolt in surprise.

"Mom," Dylan said brightly. "Can I have some ice cream?"

My head snapped around, as I shut the browser window. It was a nonsensical reaction, there was nothing revealing on the screen, my son couldn't see it anyway and even if he could, he certainly wasn't close enough to read. "How many times have I told you about knocking on that door before you come in," I grumbled, pushing myself off the chair and moving toward him.

"I did," he replied.

"Well, I didn't say 'come in'," I said, coaxing him around with a light touch at his shoulder.

He followed my silent guiding without hesitation or argument. "I'm sorry," he continued. "Can I have some ice cream, though?" he quickly added, returning to his primary concern.

"Not right now," I responded, walking down the hall with him.

"Ahhh, Mom," he moaned loudly. "Please!" he begged, turning to me and pressing his hands together in front of his chest. "Please, please, please," he rapidly added, his eyes taking on that dolefully expression he was so very good at.

Shaking my head apologetically, I hustled him ahead of me and we descended the stairs. "Maybe," I softly suggested, but before I could get the rest of the sentence out, my young son was already punching the air furiously.

"Yes!" he yelled delightedly.

"Maybe," I repeated, stressing the word this time. "If you eat all your dinner and promise to go to bed on time, I'll see what I can do about the ice cream."

"I love you, Mom," he said, turning his big brown eyes to me and grinning broadly. It was his standard way of trying to keep me sweet. His father used to do something similar when we were younger.

With the promise of ice cream, dinner was a much smoother affair than usual and I made a mental note to use bribery more often. All three children, even Kate, ate every last piece of their meal, including the greens that typically got pushed around until I got tired of trying to coax them into a mouth. Lizzie offered to help me clear away, which was no doubt a ploy to get an extra-large scoop, but it was appreciated nonetheless.

Putting them to bed that night, I spent a little longer looking at their adorable, peaceful faces. They were growing so quickly, time had been passing me by and I'd been largely oblivious to it. The shock of Paul's infidelity had caused me to put my existence into some sort of perspective. Almost thirty, and all I had to show for those years were the three kids who meant the world to me. Of course, they made me want to tear my hair out at times, but I couldn't imagine life without their mischievous charm. I wouldn't want to live in a world without them in it, my children were the only thing that made life make sense.

Closing Lizzie and Dylan's doors, and leaving Kate's fractionally ajar so she still had a little light from the hallway, I walked slowly back to my own bedroom. With a renewed sense of purpose, I settled in front of the computer screen and opened the email I'd received earlier that evening.

Hi,

I'm David, I read your advertisement and wondered if you're free on Saturday night. I know it's a bit short notice, but I have an unplanned stop in the state and I hate to be alone. Would love to learn more about you, and maybe see a picture? If you'd like to know what I look like, just say the word.

I leaned back for a moment, as the reality of what I'd done, and was planning to do, sunk in. Paul wasn't coming home until Sunday afternoon, so I certainly had the night free. However, I hadn't been expecting things to happen so quickly. I'd thought it would be at least a month, and probably much more, before I was actually working. I hadn't really had a chance to mentally prepare.

In retrospect, no matter how long it had taken, I know I would never have been prepared. It simply isn't the sort of thing that can be prepared for. But, at the time, part of me was arguing that I just needed a few weeks to really adjust to the prospect of selling my body.

However, something overrode that instinct, because I was already opening the many files of photographs we had stored on the computer. I managed to find a couple of me dressed in an evening gown at some fancy function Paul's company had organized six months previously. Choosing the one I liked best, I carefully cropped my husband out of the image, before attaching it to a new email.

I wrote a quick message, telling him that I was available if he was still interested and that I didn't need to know what he looked like.

As I clicked on 'send', I told myself his appearance didn't matter. However, I knew that my subconscious choice had been more to do with ignorance being bliss. If he was in his sixties or seventies, with a beer gut and tobacco stained teeth, the anticipation of spending the night with him would be filled with even more dread than it already was. Sex, for me, had always been inextricably linked with love. It had never been purely physical, and because Paul was my first and only lover, it had always been with someone I trusted. The thought of giving myself to a stranger; a man about whom I knew nothing and who didn't care about me, was entirely foreign and caused me to shudder.

However, I was forced to remind myself that that wasn't completely true. I no longer knew Paul and, for the last few months at least, he'd stopped caring about me. The last time we'd had sex was certainly evidence of that fact. Was offering my body to David really any different than the last time I'd been to bed with my own husband?

It only took a few minutes for him to write again.
Hey,
Thanks for getting in touch. You're a very beautiful woman, and I am definitely interested in enjoying the pleasure of your company on Saturday. You haven't mentioned fee, but it's not a problem. Whatever you charge, I'm happy to pay it.
I'm staying at the Hyatt, room 405. If you could be here at about 8pm, that would be good. Let me know. Thanks!

The Escort Next Door

Before I had time to talk myself out of it, I wrote a reply confirming that I would be there at eight o'clock.

Breathing rapidly, as I pushed the chair away from the desk, I realized that it was done. I was really going to go through with it. I had just two days to arrange a babysitter and get myself ready for what would be the most bizarre date of my life. I quickly made a list of all the things that needed to be done; my legs, although always smoothly shaved, would probably need waxing; my small, neat patch of pubic hair would have to go, too. I'd never favored the Brazilian style, but I understood enough about what was popular among men to know that the hairless look would be expected. My nails required a fresh manicure; hair needed styling; and my tan lines from wearing a bikini had to be removed.

In short, I had to look perfect. There was a lot of work to be done.

Chapter Eight

First Times A Charm

Nervous doesn't begin to describe how I felt as I walked down the hotel corridor. The backs of my legs shook so much that they felt weak, and I must have looked a bit like a newborn deer. Having felt so confident that I could go through with the night, I suddenly knew that it was nothing but bravado; intended only to convince myself.

Who was I kidding?

Having only ever slept with one man, I was almost as inexperienced as they come. Even when we were engaged and first married, Paul and I were never particularly adventurous in the bedroom. If this man had some peculiar tastes or fetishes, would I know what to do? Even if he didn't want something weird, would I be able to please him?

"Oh shit," I whispered, seriously contemplating turning around and bolting back to the elevator. "Oh shit, oh shit," I breathed. Halting the movement of my feet, I forced myself to breathe deeply. Smoothing my hands down the skirt of my red cocktail dress, I released a steady, slow exhale. I glanced down at my cleavage which was thrust up by a brand new bra I'd bought the day before. My legs were covered in black stockings and my feet securely tucked into four-inch stilettos. Flicking my newly wavy hair off my shoulder, I swallowed the anxious lump in my throat. "Pull yourself together," I softly mumbled.

When the temptation to turn back crept higher, I reminded myself why I was there. This was never about doing something that I wanted to, but what I felt I had to do. It was about putting my own fears and prudish concerns aside, because the end would justify the means.

Before I'd ordered them to do so, my feet were once more moving. The thoughts that had been racing discordantly through my head stopped and focused on the door numbers, until I reached '405'.

Quickly moistening my lips, I lifted my hand with the fingernails colored the same shade of red as my dress, and tapped softly on the door. I counted the deep thuds of my heart, while I waited for an answer. There were twelve. And then, slowly and gently the door was pulled open.

The man was much younger than I had expected, he must have been somewhere in his mid-thirties. He had dark, almost jet black hair that was cut in a neat Ivy League style, with a side parting. He was clean shaven, with soft features and dark brown eyes under quite long black lashes. As he looked at me, he smiled a little lopsided grin. "Hi," he greeted warmly, pulling the door open wider.

"Hi," I echoed, my eyes now taking in the view of the rest of his body. He was around six feet something, with strong, broad shoulders. He was wearing pinstriped black pants and a white dress shirt, with the cuffs undone.

"I'm David," he said, continuing to smile, as he moved to one side of the entry way and gestured an open hand into the room.

"Thank you," I nodded, managing a nervy smile in return as I stepped across the threshold. "I'm Arianna," I murmured, remembering to use the name I'd chosen for my call girl persona, rather than my real one. All the girls used fake names, most of them were tacky: Destinee, Lotus, Candy that kind of thing. I wanted something that sounded a little exotic and mysterious, but was still classy. I unconsciously drew in a breath as I passed him and was met with the earthy, spicy scent of whatever aftershave he'd just used. Swallowing, I silently reminded myself that it didn't matter what he smelled or looked like. I was here to do a job.

I couldn't help but feel grateful that he was attractive, though. Faking an interest in him would be made easier by the fact he was easy on the eyes.

"Can I get you a drink?" he asked, closing the door behind him.

I stopped in the room's small living space. It wasn't quite a suite, but there were two comfortable chairs and a coffee table, with a brand new TV on the wall and a minibar in the corner. Beyond that, in the open plan space was the bed. It was a king size, with crisp white sheets, four plump pillows and a beige bed scarf with the Hyatt Regency logo embroidered in the corner. "Umm, yes, please," I managed to softly mumble, remembering that he had asked me a question.

"What can I get you?" I added, already moving to the minibar. "I'm on vodka myself," he said pointing to the one liter bottle of Smirnoff that was clearly not the hotels. "But you can have whatever you like."

"Vodka's fine," I quickly stated. With my rising nerves, the stronger the alcohol, the better.

"Great," he nodded. "Take a seat," he urged, grasping two shot glasses and the bottle.

As I settled into one of the armchairs, keeping a hand on the hem of my dress to stop it riding too high, he took the few strides toward me and tossed himself into the other seat. With a tired sigh, he slipped the glasses onto the table and began unscrewing the bottle.

"So, umm," I softly mumbled, trying to think of something to say. "What brings you here?"

"Oh, just work," he shrugged. "I was supposed to be heading back yesterday, but my office messed up the arrangements and I had to stay longer than planned."

"I see," I nodded, watching him pour some of the crystal clear liquid into each shot glass. "Sorry to hear that."

"It's ok," he quickly insisted. "I'm kind of glad now. If I'd gone home Friday, I would have never had the opportunity to meet you," he smoothly said, placing the bottle down and lifting his glass as if to toast.

Carefully, I reached for my own drink and lifted it to his. We clinked the edges of the glasses together, before both swallowing the shot whole. It instantly brought a flush of tears to my eyes and a burning to my throat which I tried to mask, but a cough erupted despite my efforts.

"Okay?" he asked, chuckling.

"Yeah," I assured him, hoarsely.

He grinned skeptically, before accepting my word with a brief nod. "Well," he sighed, lifting himself from the chair just enough to reach into his back pocket. "I said money wasn't an object, but I'd like to get it out of the way, if that's all right with you," he said, pulling the wallet out and flipping it open.

"Sure," I replied.

"That way, we can get on with enjoying the night, huh?"

"Right," I agreed. "Umm, exactly what services do you want from me?" I wondered, embarrassment causing my cheeks to warm. I hoped he might think the reddening was caused by the drink.

"I was hoping you'd be able to spend about six hours with me," he unabashedly said. "Err, you offer full sex, right?"

My mouth suddenly went very dry and I could only nod in response.

"Well, I don't want anything too strange or out of the ordinary," he added. "I guess it's called the umm, girlfriend experience?" he finished with a crease of his eyebrow.

The Escort Next Door

Again, I nodded, my throat unwilling to cooperate in the making of any sounds. I'd seen the phrase 'girlfriend experience' on the many escort ads I'd seen online. And had been able to create an idea of what that would entail. I was beyond grateful that David didn't have an unusual fetish he wished to act out with me. Girlfriend experience was probably something I could just about manage.

"So?" he uttered, his thumb slipping over a large wedge of bills.

"Oh, sorry," I blurted shaking my head and realizing that this had been leading to me giving him a figure for my services. "Well, that'll be...errr... $1800." I spoke so haltingly and anxiously that I was worried my inexperience would be obvious to him.

He said nothing, while he flicked through the bills and then pulled out a fistful of them. Silently, he placed the cash on the table, before getting up and replacing his wallet in his pants. "Now," he smiled, "that's out of the way, we can concentrate on having a good time. Would you like something to eat?" he offered, visibly relaxing into the chair.

The casual way he'd dealt with the payment seemed so strange to me, and yet it was obviously necessary to separate the transaction and the 'good time'. "Sounds great," I replied, forcing a broad smile. In truth, I was so scared I didn't think I'd be able to keep anything down. But if he wanted to have dinner, then it was my job to ensure he got what he wanted. Reaching forward I scooped the cash off the table and slipped it into my purse.

"You want to go down to the restaurant?" he asked, tipping his head to the door. "Or should we just get some room service and eat up here?"

"Whatever you'd prefer," I offered warmly.

"Hmm," he looked at me, while he thought for several seconds. "On one hand, I'd like to have you on my arm. On the other, I'd kind of like to have you to myself," he chuckled.

I felt uncomfortable not only with the way he spoke about me; as if I were a commodity, but also by the way he looked at me. It was a hungry, appreciative gaze; a look that reminded me of the way a lioness eyes her prey. Of course, on the surface, I tried to let none of those emotions show. And, I had to concede, I was a commodity of sorts. I was bought and paid for.

"I think it'll be nicer to stay up here," he eventually said, cradling the back of his head in his hands. "We can really talk," he added.

While I drained another shot glass of vodka, David called down to room service and ordered for us both. I don't even remember what I had, I know I didn't spend long choosing, sure that I wouldn't touch any of it any way.

However, by the time the meal arrived, I'd had another shot and was beginning to feel much more relaxed.

David had professed an interest in learning more about me, but I'd successfully been vague in most of my answers and flipped the questions back to him. As he talked about his career as head of a sales team for a pharmaceutical company, I almost forgot the circumstances under which were we meeting.

"What about free time?" I asked, unconsciously sticking my fork into a piece of ravioli. "Any hobbies?"

"Ha," he exhaled. "What free time?" He was quiet for a moment, as he poured himself another glass of the red wine he'd order with the meal. "It feels like I'm always working, that's certainly what my ex thought."

"Oh, I'm sorry," I quickly apologized when I noted the sadness in his eyes.

"Don't be," he dismissed with a wave of his free hand. "It's not your fault." Carefully placing the bottle back down, he picked up his glass and lifted it to his lips, flashing me a smile before taking a mouthful. "But it's been tough since she left," he admitted. "My ridiculously busy schedule makes it impossible to meet anyone and I'm the kind of person that hates to be alone, you know?"

I nodded, remembering what he'd written in his first email. However, it seemed insane to me that a man like him would need to hire the services of an escort. He was young, handsome and charming. There would be any number of women who would be happy to have a one-night stand with him if that's all he could commit to.

However, his desires for the evening came back to the forefront of my mind: the girlfriend experience. He didn't want a one-night stand per se, it wasn't about a quick roll in the hay. He wanted companionship, he wanted to spend this time talking, sharing some laughs and for all intents and purposes, pretending we'd known each other for much longer than we had. If he just wanted a fuck, he could have gone down to the bar and picked up a girl or headed out on the streets to find a hooker. In fact, he could even have demanded that I get my clothes off as soon as I'd walked in the door.

"You're a sweet man," I told him, unaware of a compulsion to do so. The alcohol had loosened me up just enough to prevent my self censor from working properly. "I mean, someday a girl is going to be very lucky to have you."

The Escort Next Door

He grinned, as he lifted his napkin and wiped the sides of his mouth. "I'm sure you've heard this a lot," he responded, tossing the napkin onto his empty plate and leaning back in his chair. "But you are an incredibly sexy woman."

I actually felt myself blushing and quickly glanced down to avoid his eyes. The truth was, I hadn't heard it a lot. Paul had said it twice, maybe three times, the whole time I'd known him. "Thank you," I gracelessly mumbled.

Suddenly, David was getting to his feet. He moved around the small table until he reached my side. There, he sank into a crouched position. Still, I couldn't bring myself to look at his face. And this was not something that went unnoticed.

Slowly, he crooked his warm index finger beneath my chin and coaxed my hand around. "The fact that hearing how sexy you are embarrasses you," he said, a teasing grin quirking the corners of his mouth, "makes you even sexier."

"I...I..." I stammered, shaking my head slightly. The next time I opened my mouth, nothing came out. It didn't have the chance. David's lips were unexpectedly melded to mine. He softly moved them, the tip of his tongue occasionally darting out to take a taste of my lip. For a long second the shock of his rapid movement startled me into stillness. However, as he slowly caressed my mouth with his own, I surrendered myself to the feeling. With a soft moan, I parted my lips and understanding the unintelligible call, his tongue slipped quickly over mine.

Even as it deepened, the kiss remained soft and exploratory. Nevertheless, it was doing entirely unexpected things to me. A warmth was spreading through my abdomen, which I tried to rationalize was from the wine and shots of vodka consumed earlier. I could never have admitted it, not even to myself, at the time, but I was enjoying that kiss. David was good; gentle, but with just the right amount of pressure. His tongue roamed playfully, rather than aggressively and he tasted nice; a mixture of Merlot and tomato pasta sauce.

What's more, I was excited by the promise of where the kiss would lead.

Chapter Nine

Not Just A Job

I don't recall how I went from sitting at the table to laying on the bed. I do know that my head was swimming and it wasn't just thanks to my old friend the fermented potato.

David's mouth was still moving leisurely over mine, occasionally sucking my lower lip between his teeth. He was lying next to me on his side, pressing the length of his body to mine, while one arm draped across me and the hand gently caressed my hip.

By that stage, I was beginning to return his kiss with an enthusiasm I didn't have to fake. One of my hands had unconsciously smoothed up his chest and curled over his shoulder, while the other snaked around the back of his head and was pulling him that little bit closer. As I tightened my fingers, gripping a handful of his smooth, thick hair, a guttural groan reverberated from his open mouth to mine.

Fluidly, he eased his hand over the curve of my pelvis and began to confidently stroke his way down my thigh. When he reached my knee, he hooked his fingers behind my leg and pulled it upward. As his tongue slipped carefully over the roof of my mouth, he tugged my leg around his waist and placed the weight of his upper body on top of mine.

With a subtle, easy movement his thigh glided between my legs and the warmth of his flesh, even through clothing, caused my hips to jolt in search of a more satisfying contact.

With a noisy unclasping of wet mouths, he tenderly released his lips from mine and took several deep breaths. "You're so beautiful," he quietly said, his dangerously dark eyes staring intently at my face.

Even if my brain had been capable of coherent thought, I wouldn't have known what to say in response. But with his fingers slowly curling around to my inner thigh and edging their way higher, it was all I could do to remember to breathe.

In the silent room, there were three sounds that would otherwise have gone unnoticed; David's slightly labored breathing; my irregularly pounding heart and the soft grazing of large, masculine fingers moving over sheer nylon.

When he reached the lace tops of my stockings, the corners of his mouth twitched in a smile. Delicately, he traced the intricate swirling pattern with the backs of his fingers. "Do you mind if we leave these on?" he asked, his voice suddenly a pitch lower than it had been before.

"Of...of course," I hoarsely responded, my eyelids flickering as the sensation he was creating on my inner thigh became enough to make me grip my bottom lip between my teeth. As he began to move again, creeping ever higher, the scorching heat of his touch seemed to burn the naked flesh of my upper thigh. It caused me to jump and he instantly withdrew his fingers.

"I'm sorry," he said, smiling warmly.

"No, no," I quickly spoke over his apology. "Don't stop, I just...umm," My chest began to move rapidly, as I got lost in his warm, gentle eyes. "It felt good," I eventually whispered.

His face swept closer and his eyelids drifted closed before his lips melded to mine in a more insistent and passionate kiss. It was as if he'd gained in confidence, and as his tongue entwined with mine, his fingers resumed their journey up my inner thigh.

My brain could not keep up with what was happening or, more importantly, with the reactions my body was having to his actions. As the tip of his fingers reached the crease of my groin, and my hips bucked in response, I realized I no longer had any control.

He slipped his finger to the edge of my panties, and carefully worked his way beneath the lacy, black fabric.

Whimpering, I automatically opened my legs wider, as the soft pads of two fingers massaged the freshly waxed flesh of my outer lips.

Lifting his face from mine, David's eyes sparkled. "Arianna," he tenderly said, as he drew his fingers between my folds and found me damp. "You feel so good."

This was nothing like I'd expected. I'd assumed a client would be solely interested in getting his pleasure, possibly at the expense of an escort, but certainly with no thought for sensitivity or sensuality – the things that were perceived as purely feminine desires.

"Oh, God," he groaned, his index finger circling the rim of my entrance.

My back arched and my mouth fell open with a quiet sigh of need, while my hands gripped him more tightly. Only Paul had ever touched my sex, only Paul had ever entered me. Before that night, I'd believed that the touch of any other man would feel wholly wrong; that my body would reject the prospect and the whole ordeal would be forgettable at best and painful at worst. In fact, the reality was more exhilarating and arousing than I ever could have imagined.

David wasn't treating me like a cheap whore nor was he behaving like a stranger who simply wanted to take something from me. And yet, on some level, I still felt sluttish and rather than wanting to run from that sensation I yearned for more.

"Arianna," he whispered, his face coming back to mine and light kisses being placed along my jaw. "I know you said strictly protected sex," he mumbled quietly, his lips tickling the top of my neck. "But how do you feel about oral?"

My eyes opened sharply and I was abruptly pulled from the sexy haze I'd been lounging in. Now, it seemed I was required to actually do something. It was a harsh reminder of the fact I wasn't there to enjoy myself. It was work. "Umm," I blabbered, while I tried to organize my thoughts.

"It's just not the same with something between us," he continued, rising his head and peering down at me. "And not that you have any reason to trust me, but I promise I'm safe."

"I trust you," I breathlessly replied, unsure why I felt so certain I could. Nevertheless, I believed him.

"So, it's okay?" he asked, smiling hopefully.

His index finger was still circling my sex in slow, smooth, hypnotic motions. In that instant, I think I may have said 'yes' to whatever he asked. "All right," I nervously offered, pushing myself into a sitting position.

Fellatio was not something I'd had much experience in. Paul had always wanted me to deep throat him and, after a few failed attempts, he decided he'd rather not bother with it at all. I was anxious about my ability to pleasure a man with my mouth, it had certainly never done much for my husband.

David, oblivious to my concerns, was also pushing himself into a seated position. Flashing a sexy grin at me, he placed both hands on my legs and lifted himself between them. "Just relax," he softly instructed, his hands smoothing up my thighs and pushing my dress up with them. Carefully, he placed his thumbs in the elastic of my underwear and began to edge it off my hips.

"I..." I mumbled. "I thought you meant," I added, fumbling gracelessly with my words.

"Oh," he chuckled, sliding my panties over my knees and smoothing them all the way to my ankles. "This is okay, right?" he added, carefully lifting one of my stilletoed feet and tugging my underwear completely from me.

"Whatever you want," I nodded, as my panties were removed from my opposite foot and tossed on the bed by his side.

His large hands returning to my waist, he encouraged me to lie back, while inching the dress just a little higher still.

I settled anxiously onto the mattress, my eyes not daring to look down at what he was doing. I was completely exposed to his hungry gaze; his silence and lack of movement as he seemed to carefully take in every detail of me, was unnerving.

However, eventually, he did move. Lifting one of my legs, he placed the knee on his shoulder, before shuffling closer to me. Turning his head to the side, he brushed his lips across the naked skin at the top of my stockings, creating sparks of electricity that shot up to the juncture of my thighs. He kissed his way steadily higher until, as if in slow motion, his tongue began to push its way between my plump folds.

"Ohh," I moaned, my voice shaking and body convulsing slightly.

David responded with a rapid lick upward to my clit. It was so sensitive that the touch of his tongue made me feel as though I had been electrocuted and I shuddered beneath him. With a soft grunt, he drew lazy circles across my tight bud, surprising me when he suddenly slipped the tip of one finger inside my entrance.

"God," I yelped, unable to prevent the reflex to buck my hips.

It might have been no more than my imagination, but I was sure I could feel his lips smiling, as he gradually lapped more feverishly at my clitoris. Desperately, my hands darted down to his head and ran restlessly across his scalp. I had never experienced anything quite so intense in my life. I could feel the heat flushing my face, as I panted shallow breathes and exhaled weak groans and mutters of pleasure.

As he mixed up the rhythm and movement of his tongue, drawing long strokes rather than focusing solely on my tiny bud of nerve endings, he pushed his finger a little deeper. With a slight curve of his finger, he began rubbing at the front wall of my passage, causing yet more strong quakes of ecstasy to rock me.

I watched the top of his head as he slowly made his way back to my clit and began to move in strong, purposeful jerks. As his smooth, skillful tongue strummed at my engorged flesh, his finger rubbed harder and faster at the spongy skin inside my sex.

The ascent was quick; the heat inside me rocketed and my head span violently. When I felt that I was about to explode, I sucked in a deep breath and held it firmly in my lungs. My trembling limbs suddenly locked tight, my thighs clamped around David's head, my fingers seized around handfuls of hair. As the molten pleasure sent warmth spilling through my body, my mouth fell open and I could not hold back the screeches of sheer joy. Meanwhile, my hips swayed, pressing more firmly against his mouth in an attempt to make the feeling last forever.

But it didn't last forever. All too quickly, the feeling seeped to my extremities and dissipated through the tips of my fingers and toes. With that came a relaxing of the spasms that had claimed every inch of me and I finally released him. My head dropping back onto the bed, I gasped for air.

I was unaware of David slowly rising from his position between my legs and drawing his upper body level with mine. "You taste incredible," he hummed, his lips close to my face.

Sluggishly opening my eyes, I found his features hanging a couple of inches over mine. His lips and the skin around them were moist and shiny from my arousal; his hair was mussed from where I'd viciously grabbed it and the sides of his face were a little red from my impersonation of a boa constrictor.

"Oh," I muttered, my post-orgasm vision taking a while to focus. "I'm sorry, I didn't mean to-"

"It's fine," he dismissed quickly. "It was a genuine reaction," he added. "I love that."

"Well," I quietly hedged, my eyes leaving his and drifting to his mouth. "You're very good," I whispered, unsure whether I'd said the words aloud or if they'd remained in my head.

He laughed a little self-effacingly, his lower half gently pressing against mine. "I don't know about that," he mumbled. "But you're incredibly responsive."

I felt my eyebrows creep upward, as the swell of his groin suddenly made itself known against my inner thigh. I'd guessed he must have been aroused, but not having noticed the evidence of it, the suddenness of his shockingly hard member caught me by surprise.

"I want you," he whispered.

"I'm all yours," I replied breathlessly.

He lunged his head forward, claiming my mouth in a kiss that now tasted of both him and me. It was brief, but spoke of the heights of his desire. Quickly, he was pushing himself up, his hands already unfastening his shirt.

I followed him, sitting up and grabbing the bottom of his shirt. I rapidly unclasped some of the lower buttons, my shaky fingers meeting him somewhere in the middle. We both giggled as we fought over the last fastener. He won, making short work of the final button and peeling the white, crisp shirt off his shoulders.

He was very well built, with chiseled chest muscles and washboard abs. Unlike Paul, David had a neat pattern of dark hair that began at his collarbone and spread across his broad chest muscles. At his abdomen, a strip of finer hair drew a line between his abs and disappeared beneath the waistband of his pants.

As I realized I was staring at the incredibly sculptured, masculine torso before me, another revelation hit me. I'd always believed I preferred a smooth, hairless chest, but there was something so rugged and masculine about David's torso. Something a little feral; animalistic and unspeakably sexy.

When my eyes finally made it back to his face, I found him smiling at me. "Will I do?" he asked, with a great deal of humor and just a small degree of nervousness in his tone.

"Oh, yeah," I grinned. "You'll definitely do," I added, my hands reaching for his belt buckle and beginning to wrench it open.

Carefully, he took hold of my wrists, stilling my hands before peeling them away from him. When I followed his silent instructions, he gradually released me and in response to my confused and startled expression, he reached both arms around my back. With the finger and thumb of his right hand, he took hold of the tiny zipper at the back of my dress and leisurely pulled it down. As the bodice began to slacken, he used his left hand to coax the strap off my shoulder. As he did, he dipped his head forward and kissed the small piece of skin it had once covered.

I shrugged out of the opposite side, causing the front of my dress to fall in a puddle at my middle. The tiny straps had meant I'd had to forgo a bra and my breasts were now naked to his scrutiny. His eyes actually moved steadily between my bosom and my face, locking on the latter as he cupped one hand to each breast.

His fingers moved smoothly, massaging the globes of flesh with just the right amount of pressure. His thumbs meanwhile, rubbed teasingly over my nipples, prompting me to mewl plaintively. All too soon, his hands were gone, slipping down my torso and pushing the dress down. I lifted my butt, helping him ease it off my hips, then he swept it down my legs and over my feet with ease.

With the exception of my stockings and stilettos, I was completely nude. And I realized, as I glanced down my body, that the soft skin around my sex was glistening with the same fluid that had been spread around Ben's mouth.

The Escort Next Door

But that didn't seem to bother him. He quickly shuffled back, slipping off the bed and reaching for the cabinet on the right side. Yanking open the top drawer, he enclosed something in his hand, before quickly closing it again. With his free fingers, he unbuckled his belt with ease and unfastened the fly of his pants. With the help of gravity, they quickly dropped to the floor and he kicked them, and his shoes, off.

"I'm sorry," he said, gripping the thick elastic waistband of his boxer briefs and forcing them over his hips. "But I need you right now, I can't wait any longer."

Chapter Ten

The Escort Next Door

My jaw slackened as his underwear was pushed down his legs and his manhood sprung free. His circumcised penis was huge; thick, long and perfectly smooth. It was rock hard, which was obvious even without touching him.

"It's all right," he said calmly. "I've got a rubber," he added, holding up the thing he'd retrieved from the drawer just seconds before.

I tried to relax, to ensure that he didn't realize my expression of mild alarm was for a completely different reason. I forced a smile, as I watched him slide the condom down to the base of his shaft with practiced ease.

He then bent at the waist scooping his boxers and socks off, before moving back to the bed. I scooted into the middle of the mattress, one hand leaning down and grabbing the large heel of one shoe.

"No," he quickly urged. "Leave those on, too."

"Okay," I nodded. I was expecting him to climb onto the bed and place himself between my slightly parted legs.

However, he simply sat on the edge, turning his head over his shoulder at me. "Come here," he encouraged with a playful jerk of his head.

I followed his instructions, sitting up then rolling onto my knees and shuffling across the bed toward him. As soon as I was within reach, he wrapped one arm around me and pulled me closer. The other hand curled over my hip, the fingers reaching my ass. With both arms able to guide me, he compelled me to lift one leg over his so I was straddling him.

My eyes were fixed on the hard rod between his legs. The rounded head, beneath a thin layer of cream latex, that was straining toward my sex. Using his shoulders for balance, I slowly peered into his face.

"Please, Arianna," he groaned, his hips involuntary jerking.

Taking a steady, slow inhale, I realized that there was no turning back. I had passed the point of no return. Of course, what I wouldn't have admitted then was that I would not have turned back even if I could have. Forcing myself to breathe calmly, I slowly lowered my hips. David's hands were sliding serenely over my lower back, occasionally dipping to caress the curve of my buttocks.

I closed my eyes and tipped my head back, as I felt his domed tip begin to force its way inside me. I held still, giving my entrance a chance to adjust to the unfamiliarly significant girth. However, instead of the discomfort I expected to experience as he entered, the sensation was satisfying. Ready for him, my body wanted to be stretched and I instinctively sank deeper.

"Ugh," he groaned, his hands clasping my buttocks tightly. "Yeah, that's good."

"Hmm," I moaned luxuriously, inching further and further until my outer lips met his firm pubic bone. Startled, I opened my eyes and snatched a glance down to our joined bodies. I was amazed that he was buried to the hilt, he was completely sheathed within me; filling me in a way that felt unbearably good.

It obviously felt pretty good for him, too. His pupils were dilated, he was gasping heavily and his brow had a few beads of sweat. As he tipped his face to the ceiling, I watched his throat flex as he swallowed.

Running my right hand down the length of his arm, I clasped his fingers between mine and lifted his hand to my mouth. Moistening my lips, I guided two of his fingers over my tongue, closing my mouth around them. When this caused his hips to thrust against mine, I sucked hard on them.

"Arianna," he whispered, his head thrusting forward. His tongue moved frantically between my breasts, following the curve of one before moving to the center and latching onto the nipple. He gently grazed it with his teeth before tapping it with the tip of his tongue. It grew harder under his attention, painfully so.

"Ahh," I cried, releasing his hand. Writhing, I rubbed my slick clit against his rigid body. I couldn't hold back any longer. With a suddenness that surprised even me, I forced my thighs into action, lifting my body, before hurriedly slapping back down. This time, as his dick slid into my wet passage, it seemed to go deeper. "Ugh," I grunted as my ass slapped against his thighs.

David tried to keep his mouth on my breasts, lapping and sucking as best he could at the moving target.

Needing the leverage, I put my hands back on his shoulder and began to bounce up and down on his thick, stiff shaft. As he buried his face in my cleavage,

I wrapped my hands around his head, enjoying the feel of his panted breath against my skin.

My own lungs were expelling air in excited shrieks and squeals. Soon, my legs no longer had the strength to lift me to the top of his penis. Instead, I could only manage feeble shallow thrusts.

David began to help me, his hands guiding my hips and supporting some of my weight. However, his motions had become equally rapid and uncoordinated. As his grunts and my cries rose and combined, he lifted his face to mine.

I peered down at his sweaty expression, my breasts jiggling around so violently that they were slapping against the underside of his chin.

"Ugh, God. You're so hot," he panted. "Arianna, you're...you're so fucking hot."

"Ahhh," I cried, an extra strong jolt against his pubic bone sending waves of orgasm through me.

As my internal muscles spasmed and clamped him, David began to desperately buck beneath me. "Yes," he groaned. "Ugh, Christ!" His hands tightened at my hips, fingertips digging into the thin flesh.

Aftershocks caused me to jerk and writhe against him for several more seconds, while our pounding hearts began to slow. I could feel his pulse pressed against my right breast and remember marveling, just for a moment, at the fact our hearts seemed to be racing in time with each other.

Eventually, I grew still. My butt falling to his lap and my sex pressed as close to his as I could get. My arms were wrapped tightly around him, unwilling or perhaps unable to let go. His softening shaft was still tucked snugly within me and I was in no hurry to break the spell of calm, comfort and serenity that had descended over the two of us.

"Are you okay?" he softly asked, his hands making lazy patterns up my spine.

With a ridiculous smile on my face, I nodded, knowing he would feel the movement against the side of his face. "I'm good," I said, my voice thick and weary. "Was it okay for you?" I quickly added, remembering suddenly that I'd been moving to the demands of my own body; chasing an orgasm for myself without the conscious awareness that the only person that mattered was him – the paying customer.

"Are you kiddin'?" he laughed. "God," he sighed. "That was incredible."

"Are you sure?" I insisted, releasing my hold of him enough to tip back and look at his face.

"Arianna," he said, shaking his head with amusement. "I haven't had an orgasm like that in a long time."

"Me neither." The words slipped out before I had a chance to hold them back. "I mean," I added, wanting to backtrack, but unsure how to without offending him. Giving up the search for something that would make me sound more experienced, I shrugged. "I guess, I mean exactly what I said," I sighed. "It's been a long time since I've felt like that."

"You know," he said, with his lopsided smile. "Coming from any other woman who does what you do, I would think that you were just telling the client what he wants to hear," he continued. "But I believe you. And I can't tell you how good that makes me feel."

"Really?" I asked, cocking my head to one side. The fact that we were still joined, still naked, entwined in each other's arms didn't seem in the least bit odd. Instead, talking to him like that felt like the most natural thing in the world. I was more relaxed than I'd been all day, more relaxed than I'd felt for months, maybe even years.

"A woman's orgasm," he began, his eyes drifting to a spot on the wall behind me, "is beyond beautiful. It's beyond sexy. It's one of those rare special, fleeting moments when life seems to make sense; my life seems to make sense, you know?" he finished, nervously searching my face for understanding.

"Yeah," I offered quietly, "I guess I do."

"What are we all here for if it's not to give and receive pleasure from each other?" he added. "I don't mean just sex, and I don't mean seeking pleasure when it's going to hurt someone else. But those moments that make us feel alive, those are what are precious."

I nodded silently, ruminating on what he'd said. In a nutshell, he'd summed up the job of an escort. Companionship was a form of pleasure; sexual gratification was quite obviously a source of it, too. The role of an escort was to bring some of those precious experiences to another human being.

I wasn't naïve enough to believe that all men who hired call girls were as nice or as affectionate as David, but maybe they weren't all as sex-crazed and selfish as I'd assumed either.

"Anyway," he said, nudging my thoughts aside. "I guess, I'd better," he muttered, tilting his head toward his groin, "take that off."

"Oh, right," I blurted, suddenly remembering the condom that was still covering him and now filled. "Then, I guess I'd better get up," I stated obviously, sliding my hands back onto his shoulders, which were clammy with drying sweat, and pushing my lower half off his lap.

His hands remained securely on my waist as I rocked back and placed my feet on the ground.

"I...umm," he grinned, his eyes moving appreciatively up and down my body. "I hope to make you come like that again before the night is out."

"Huh?" I quizzically muttered, glancing at the digital clock on the bedside. There were another three hours of David's time with me. Did it make me even more of a whore that I smiled like the Cheshire cat when I realized that?

***

It was almost three in the morning when I eventually got home. I'd ended up staying an extra half an hour with David. It was time I'd assured him he didn't need to pay for, especially since he'd promised to hire me again next time he was in town. In fact, he'd even suggesting flying me across the country to spend evenings with him elsewhere. With the kids and trying to keep my moonlighting secret, out of state trips would have proven difficult. However, I was certainly keen and said I'd think about it. In any case, he insisted on paying for the additional thirty minutes, and while his hand was in his wallet he grabbed some cash for my cab fare.

By the time I wandered into my kitchen and poured myself a mug of herbal tea, the effects of the alcohol had well and truly worn off. However, I was not as tired as I'd expected to feel. In fact, quite the reverse, I was wide awake. I felt energized, I was on a strange kind of high, the like of which I'd never known.

Never in my wildest dreams had I expected to actually enjoy selling my body. Never had I imagined that a man who pays women for sex, could be a more tender, considerate and affectionate lover than my own husband. David was possibly better in bed than Paul had ever been; sex with him had definitely been better than the last few years with Paul.

More importantly, I told myself, I had a little over two thousand dollars in my purse. I'd need much more to be completely free of Paul, but it was a great start.

The positive experience with David had renewed my enthusiasm for the idea. Not all clients would be like him, that was obvious. But I'd learned something important about myself; I could do it. I could have sex with a stranger, sex with no real attachment. If I'd done it once, I could do it again. And, there was a chance that there were more David's out there; more men who wanted an uncomplicated evening, but who still treated women with respect. In fact, the more I thought about it, the more it occurred to me that men who use escorts do view women with respect. It's men who pick up any girl in a bar, tell her what she wants to hear, then disappears in the morning and spends the next month dodging her calls, who have little or no respect for women.

An escort's clients are, at least, honest; they're frank about what they want and they're willing to pay a fair price for a girl's time. The more I thought about it, the more I realized it wasn't anything like as sleazy and degrading as I'd first assumed. Perhaps I was just trying to make myself feel better, because I was now one of those women I'd considered degraded, but I truly believe that my eyes had been opened that night.

And that wasn't the only thing.

Sex had never been a particular preoccupation of mine. During the first stages of our adult relationship, Paul and I had sex quite frequently and I enjoyed it. I especially liked the fact that it seemed to make him so happy. However, I didn't 'get it'. I could not understand why women craved sex, why they would put themselves in dangerous situations to seek it out. It was fine; it was nice, but it wasn't the earthshaking experience so many people seemed to think.

In the most unexpected of places, my earth had been shaken. I understood it now with a clarity I could never have believed. I had left David completely satisfied, relaxed and happier than I'd felt in months. But in the quiet of my kitchen, the desire was building already. Yes, I wanted the money, I wanted to secure a future for me and the children – those were my prime concerns.

But I'd be lying if I said the thrill of what I'd done hadn't sparked a sort of addiction. I wanted more sex, uncomplicated sex with no attachments; pure pleasure without hurting anyone else.

To be continued...

Thanks for reading!!

Also by bestselling author

Clara James

~The Escort Next Door Series~

The Escort Next Door

The Escort Next Door: Captivated

The Escort Next Door: Escape

~Her Last Love Affair Series~

Her Last Love Affair

Her Last Love Affair: Breathing Without You

Her Last Love Affair: The Final Journey

To view these titles visit:
http://amzn.to/15ek5q7

Printed in Great Britain
by Amazon.co.uk, Ltd.,
Marston Gate.